KU-850-527

The
WONDERS

WITHDRAWN FOR SALE

The

WONDERS

Elena
Medel

**Translated from
the Spanish by
Lizzie Davis and
Thomas Bunstead**

PUSHKIN PRESS

Pushkin Press
71–75 Shelton Street
London WC2H 9JQ

Las maravillas © by Elena Medel Navarro, 2020
By agreement with Pontas Literary & Film Agency.

English translation © Lizzie Davis and Thomas Bunstead 2022

First published by Pushkin Press in 2022

Support for the translation of this book was provided
by Acción Cultural Española, AC/E

AC/E
ACCIÓN CULTURAL
ESPAÑOLA

1 3 5 7 9 8 6 4 2

ISBN 13: 978-1-78227-658-6

All rights reserved. No part of this publication may be reproduced,
stored in a retrieval system or transmitted in any form or by any
means, electronic, mechanical, photocopying, recording or otherwise,
without prior permission in writing from Pushkin Press

Epigraph from 'Money' by Philip Larkin, reprinted
with permission from Faber and Faber Ltd

Designed and typeset by Tetragon, London
Printed and bound by CPI Group (UK) Ltd, Croydon, CRO 4YY

www.pushkinpress.com

The
WONDERS

Clearly money has something to do with life

PHILIP LARKIN

DAY

Madrid, 2018

S HE CHECKED HER POCKETS and found nothing. Her
trouser pockets, then the ones in her jacket: not so much
as a used tissue. In her purse, nothing but a euro and a
twenty-céntimo coin. Alicia won't need any money till after
her shift ends, but it makes her uncomfortable, this feeling
of being so close to zero. I work at the train station, in one
of the sandwich and sweet shops, the one near the public
toilets: that's how she usually introduces herself. There are
no cash machines without fees in Atocha, so she gets off the
metro one stop early and looks for a branch of her bank,
withdrawing twenty euros to ease her mind. This solitary
note in her pocket, Alicia looks out at the virtually deserted
roundabout, a few cars, a few pedestrians. Shortly the sky will
start growing light. Given the choice, Alicia always takes the
late shift: that way she gets to wake up when she likes, spend
the afternoon at the shop, then go directly home. Nando
grumbles when that happens, or all the time, really, while she
claims it's better for her co-worker, who has two kids, so the
early shift suits her. But it means having the first few hours of
the day to herself, and avoiding afternoons at the bar with his

friends—who are hers, too, by default—cheap tapas, babies, dirty napkins everywhere. Alicia always thought the ritual would end when the others became parents, but they only actually stay away till the kids drop off, come straight back once they're in a deep sleep, and it upsets Nando when she tries to get out of it. At least give me that, he says. "That," sometimes meaning the whole second half of the day in the bar downstairs, and other times, travelling with him on that season's cycling tour: he rides his bike, she goes along in a car with the other women. Alicia considers the word *esposa*, meaning both "spouse" and "handcuff," and how the sound of the word and its meaning never seem more precisely linked than on those weekends: the skin on her wrists stings, as if chafed by metal. At night, in the hostel—cheap, coarse sheets—Nando bites his lip and clamps a hand over her mouth so the noise doesn't give them away, and after he's finished, asks why she always tries to avoid these trips when they do her so much good.

And so it goes on, day after night and night after day, sometimes melding into one another, day night night day, and a morning never comes when she calls in sick and just walks through the city instead, and never a night without the same recurring nightmare. Her supervisors—she's had several, always men with shirts tucked in, at first a little older than her, these days a little younger—applaud her for staying on so long, years and years in the same post. Some of them ask if she doesn't get bored selling travel kits to commuters all day long, and she tells them, no, she's happy; for her, it's enough. They appreciate that in particular: it's reassuring to hear she's happy, the sweetshop girl—Patricia, wasn't that your name? One of them wanted to know if she didn't have dreams: if you only knew, she thought—the man with the limp flashing through her thoughts, his dead body swinging in circles—while in her boss's mind she was picturing luxury urban apartments, months lounging on beaches with crystalline waters.

Early shift or late, she approaches it the same: if she works the early, she always picks Nando up afterwards or waits for him to call, or they have drinks in the bar to the soundtrack of other people's kids crying; if the late, she finds more satisfying ways to spend her time. Some mornings she puts on a little make-up, though she doesn't know what to accentuate these days—over time, fat has come to settle on her hips and thighs, and there are the rat eyes she inherited from her mother, who inherited them from her father, or so her uncle Chico claims in a tone of lament—she walks through neighbourhoods Nando never sets foot in, feigns interest in the conversation over coffee in a bar where they haven't yet managed to hire a chef, across from a butcher's that's closing down.

In the beginning, with Nando in the city, she resisted her urges, afraid she'd be found out. But then it happened one day: red tape at the social security office, a guy younger than her in the waiting room insisting on showing her the book he was reading. Alicia finds her body more and more shameful all the time, so it was a chance she seized.

The Atocha roundabout virtually deserted, not many cars, not many pedestrians: a few minutes till sunrise. On Cuesta de Moyano, the stall shutters still down, several purple dots—she can barely make them out in the distance, the women—stacking up placards near the carousel. She heard about something happening today on TV, but then she gets distracted, the walk sign comes on, she crosses over to the station, her mind on matters closer to home.

María sleeps soundly—like a log. When she retired, she put her alarm clock in a plastic bag and left it on the association's second-hand shelf for anyone who might need it. She'd gone years without using it— like everyone, she'd replaced it with the one on her mobile instead—but the gesture seemed symbolic, like something out of someone else's story: now that I won't be needing it any more, why shouldn't it be of use to someone who does, an object in another story whose protagonist leaves the house before dawn? She almost always wakes up unaided anyway, stirring when the light filters through the blinds or the person in the adjacent flat gets into the shower. They started preparing for this day months ago. Last night, signing off on WhatsApp, Laura wrote, "cant believe its really happening." At assemblies, at district meetings, María has always tried to stop the younger girls from getting too excited, but now she's excited too: my whole life, the near seventy years I've lived, it's all led to waking up today, being here at your gathering, walking beside you. They were briefed at the association: do whatever you want, a paid work strike, a consumer strike, a care strike. Choose whatever works for you, because for us it all works, and we aren't here to hand out badges for who's the best feminist. My husband will notice if I don't have a meal ready for him. Well then, Amalia, put some soup in a Tupperware and tell him he can warm it up himself. Can't he even manage that? Give him a microwave class next week, beginners' level. I have to work, I can't afford not to get paid, but I'll meet up with you later on at Atocha. Does taking care of yourself count? I'm thinking of running a hot bath before I leave the house in the morning, soaking till I wrinkle up like a prune. Sure, why not, today's about taking care of ourselves and our sisters.

The previous afternoon, several of them had met up at the association: some busied themselves making sandwiches for whoever would be out in the streets today, spreading the word to the women leaving the supermarket, and the ones who'd gone in to work; others opted not to strike, but showed up early at the headquarters to talk about events in different cities, and here in their own. Does listening to the radio count as a strike? Watching what's happening online? They uncovered a foil-wrapped tray and passed out pieces of sponge cake. They had baked empanadas, the girls made hummus and guacamole, one of the veterans dunked a spoon in the clay pot as if it were soup or custard, to jokes from the girls: that's not how you eat hummus. It seemed too modern to her, and she thought of her mother, who'd lived through the war and would never have wasted food like that: where d'you think you're from, the Nile or Carabanchel, because here in Carabanchel we put chickpeas in a stew. While they were making chorizo and salami sandwiches, cutting them into triangles, wrapping them in cling film, stacking them in the fridge to hand out the next day, María listed all the protests and strikes she hadn't taken part in: the ones against Suárez in the seventies, before the elections and then afterwards, the one against NATO, the one for pensions in '85, the strike of '88 and the two in the nineties, Iraq and the "No to War" one, the one in 2010, the two in 2012—the one here against Rajoy, and the Europe one—the freedom train, pro-choice. The Tides, remembers another girl, already university-aged, you were there for the Green Tide, and María recounts how at one of the demonstrations, a reporter asked her if she was protesting on behalf of her granddaughter, and she, not knowing how to respond, said yes, that she was, for her granddaughter and for all of her granddaughter's friends, and the girls in the younger group at the association waved at the camera without letting on that they weren't related to her. María confidently pronounced the first and last names of the men who formed part of her biography—Felipe, Boyer, Aznar—and who would never know a thing about the seventy-year-old woman who had left a half-built neighbourhood in a city in southern Spain for working-class Carabanchel, Madrid. One of Zapatero's ministers granted the association a prize, but María didn't pick it up. They gave them out in the morning and she couldn't get the time off work.

Nando pleads: at least give me that, Alicia. "That" no longer includes marriage, which Alicia agreed to because it got her that run-down apartment in that run-down neighbourhood, nor kids, which he's accepted—just about—are never going to come along. "That" means a weekend with the cycling club, pleasant landscapes in mediocre company, another few days at the beach with his mother, with whom Alicia practises the healthy art of silence; "that" is another word for Saturday night at another couple's house, or dinner at a local restaurant. Alicia had gotten herself into this—"this," not "that": Nando, living with Nando, marrying him and moulding her life to his—and refusing him children in turn obliged her to make certain daily concessions: if you want something, you have to give something up in return; if you keep something back, you have to make up for it. There's still time: what if she told him yes, OK, and if they were lucky and managed it quickly and within a year had attached a co-sleeping cradle to their bed so they could hear the wailing nice and close? How hard would it be to lose the pounds she'd gain? Would her supervisor repay her for having intoned over so many years that, no, the burger isn't included in the meal deal, or would they replace her with a girl ten years younger who cares as little as she does if she makes peanuts? Her bra damp with breast milk, her belly sagging. She'd need a new way to break the ice, since she's happy enough to say yes to men too old or too ridiculous when she finds nothing better, but she worries that not even they would want her after she'd become a mother: getting a woman with a saggy body and stretch marks is not getting lucky. Her body after giving birth: can Alicia imagine it? How does she think Nando would take it if her breasts drooped even more, if the stretch marks spread to her thighs? He'd stop using her name to speak to her—even in public he'd start calling her "Mum," as if she'd given birth to two. In the time leading up to it, Nando would refuse to have sex with her, out of fear of stunting his brilliant offspring's mind with a thrust—so that at least would be in Alicia's favour:

her transformation from wife to mother would protect her
from her husband's desire—and he would make her tea
for morning sickness those first months, bring her teething
necklaces, breastfeeding clothes. She thinks about a baby—
let's call her Little Alicia—who doesn't exist, which seems
a reason to rejoice—will she have her rat eyes or Nando's
eyes?—and then she starts trawling the internet: nursing
gowns, side-access shirts for lactating, her breasts in one of
those horrifying bras. With any luck, during her pregnancy,
Nando's eye would be caught by one of the girls who work
in the warehouse, in admin—he's mentioned several, nice
girls, very well qualified, she forgets their names—and he'd
leave her in peace for a while, a few months, the rest of her
life. What will she do with Little Alicia then, if Little Alicia
exists, if Nando's off having fun? The first idea she has is to
use her for her forays into the city: maybe a man will come
up to her hoping to help her collapse the pram, or some
lech will start a conversation while she's waiting for the
metro. How old is the little one?—Little Alicia dressed in
pink, her frills and a pearl in each earlobe ever since she was
tiny—and she'll answer enthusiastically and make something
up, while she still can, while Little Alicia neither hears nor
cares, she's not listening, all she cares about is crying and
feeding and shitting and having her nappy changed. Little
Alicia parked next to the umbrella stand, in an apartment in
Palomeras or Las Tablas, while her mother fucks a stranger
who asks for her number and for weeks afterwards will be
sending dick pics to a maths teacher in Cartagena whose
number has three or four digits in common with Alicia's.
She doesn't bother to stifle her laughter, even though the

customers can hear. And what if Little Alicia retains some image from these encounters, some sound? In the dreams her daughter has for the rest of her life, a woman's body on top of a man's, the stuccoed walls of an apartment filled with furniture three decades old, someone asking someone to go down, someone asking someone to come up, suddenly, just before waking, Little Alicia recognizing her face in the face of the woman stretched out beside a body she knows nothing of, a body that disgusts her, bathed in sweat and, for an instant, truly happy.

So did you see many women at the meetings before, María? One of the girls, virtually a teenager, asked the question innocently, a trail of red chorizo grease from her wrist to her fingertips; her hands, rough from chores since she was little, always stood out to María, who saw them as a sign that she'd end up having to use them more than her head. In spite of her youth, the things the girl said astonished María—the daughter of a friend's daughter, she told herself with a strange sense of pride—she expressed her opinions emphatically, could empathize with other people's points of view, and at the same time, there was something comforting to María in the remark, which confirmed how green the girl was: I can't believe the men wouldn't let you speak. I always went with the guys from the neighbourhood association, María explained. I started going out with one of them five or six years after I moved to Madrid. I went to those meetings to make the neighbourhood a better place: it was a rough area in those days, even more than it is now, addicts shooting up in broad daylight, right at the door to my building, and they wouldn't stop at just snatching your handbag, and then there were still whole shanty areas and, further out, the prisons. We all had the feeling that south of the river was a waste-land full of nothing and nobody. Nothing and nobody, of course, meant us. I started to think about what they were saying at the meetings, started to note down some of the writers' names they mentioned, they and other men I didn't know so well, at the meetings and the bars where we went out afterwards. I would jump from one writer to the next, and the next, and then share whatever conclusions I came to with that same man, my partner—Pedro was his name—and we'd argue about them. He'd bring them up for discussion at the next meeting, and they'd all swoon over how clever he seemed, like some academic. I kept quiet, because he made it sound better than I could ever have hoped to. I started meeting up with some women, your grandma, some other friends, in one living room or another, at my place, and that's where we'd go to talk about the topics concerning us more specifically, the things the men weren't interested in: divorce, abortion, violence, not just the physical kind, but emotional, too. Your mum started recommending books she found out about during her degree, and I kept reading and learning, and I started to see that the more I thought for myself, the more uncomfortable it made Pedro. So we, your mum and I, talked; we talked and talked like we always did, and we decided to ask the association if we could form a women's group. In their minds it was going to be a clothes and recipes swap. Well, your mum and some of her university friends moved in, and we started making a nuisance of ourselves.

The city council gave us a premises, but then took it away as soon as we complained about the lack of lighting in the park. With a bit of money we scraped together, we rented our own. I was working all hours back then, cleaning offices in Nuevos Ministerios; I'd come back and grab something to eat, a sandwich on the metro or something quick at home, not even taking time to sit down, and some nights I got out to see Pedro for a while, but I don't think I've ever been happier. Not even now that I get to sleep in, now that I spend all day at the association, and seeing all of you really helping each other out. That was the first time in my life that I felt like people were listening when I talked, respecting the things I said. And not because they wanted to get me into bed, and they'd just tuned out my voice and were hearing some far-off thing I couldn't pick up on instead, but because someone understood me, they agreed with me, they thought what I had to say was worth listening to in and of itself. There was a moment when all of that, thinking something and voicing it, doing the things I said I would, the association, seemed much more important than anything Pedro could have offered me. He wanted us to move in together, and I realized the whole thing had nothing to do with love. I wasn't someone—María—but some*thing*, and something he felt he owned: his apartment, his car, his woman. This scar—and she points to her chin, a scratch that shines on white skin—I got it hurrying off the bus one day; I tripped and fell, and he did nothing, couldn't have cared less. We lasted a year after that. So no: I mean, there were never any women like us. What do you mean, María? I mean, women who are poor. You need money even to protest.

HOME

Córdoba, 1969

THE BABY SMELLS OF CIGARETTES. The first thing
María notices when she picks Carmen up is that she
doesn't smell anything like the other babies. The neighbours' daughter, in the apartment next to her aunt and
uncle's, sometimes smells like onions, though the mother
tries to cover it up with perfume; but the little boy at her
place—the place where she works, María catches herself,
not her own, there's no such thing—is a few months older
than her daughter, and he has a sweet scent. It's hard for
María to explain—what is "a sweet scent"?—since she'd
never come across anything like it, but now she picks it out
in shops, in cafés. The neighbours' daughter plays with
the pots and pans in the afternoon, and the boy divides his
time between the cot and the Moses basket in the living
room; Carmen has her own way of moving through the
house, from the bedroom to the arms of her grandmother,
who sits at the big table. María realizes maybe the smell of
cigarettes has something to do with her family. Her mother
smokes in the kitchen; her father smokes constantly; and she
suspects that her brother Chico has taken to smoking in the

bedroom, trusting he won't be found out. Carmen smells of cigarettes; maybe it feels to María that her daughter smells of a two-room apartment, or maybe it's just the strangeness of sleeping there next to her.

Carmen turned one a few weeks ago, and María is home for the first time since she moved away: on the bus, she rehearsed the words she would use to describe the wide streets of Madrid, the gaps she would insert in place of the neighbourhoods her aunt and uncle implored her to avoid. She tried to strike up a conversation with the woman in the seat next to hers, talked about the weather and the differences between the two cities—the avenues, the areas people tell you to stay away from—but in return María got gibberish, monosyllables, one cliché or another. Downtime frightened her; she needed to fill it somehow. She fell asleep at points, or watched the landscape changing colour: the coarse yellow soil looked more and more scorched the further south they went. While her daughter naps, María tries to rest, but she only gets as far as lying down on her side, eyes open, gaze fixed on the rise and fall of her chest. She whiles the time away looking for her features in Carmen's. She'd remembered the soft little hands, but had forgotten all about the uneven chin—she has such a complex about her own. Carmen barely has any hair—it's brown, like her father's—and the little she has is so fine that María tries to avoid touching it, afraid that it might disintegrate. She's smaller than María thought—much smaller than the boy she takes care of—and her belly is still swollen. She accepts that the very pale skin must have come from her mother's side, and she has no trouble imagining her a few years younger than María is now, veins showing through on her arms and her chest. She wishes better luck on Carmen.

In her memory, the entire length of her daughter fits in her open arms; she's too big for that nowadays, and María carries her on one hip instead. It's funny, María will think many years from now, how memory generates its own fictions: how what hasn't stayed with us, because we think it insignificant or because it doesn't align with our expectations, gets filled in with what we wish had happened instead. During the day she cooks and cleans and irons and follows orders, but she sets night-time aside for memory. Before she falls asleep, she takes herself back to her parents' house, its layout: when you go inside, there's the small entryway for hanging coats, her parents' room is on the left—the wooden headboard, blinds almost always lowered. When the house was turned over to them, there was a living room in that space, and it's not hard for María to remember the hastily erected partitions. On the right is the room she shared with the siblings closer to her in age, Soledad and Chico, and in previous times, with the older ones. At the back, the kitchen with the big table, and beyond that, the backyard and the toilet, which originally had been a hole in the ground—the weight of the bucket in the corner, full to the brim with water, don't forget to empty it first and fill it up after for whoever comes next. They took apart her bed, and the girl's cot now stands in its place: the same cot where her nieces, now nearly teenagers, slept, where her little brother slept. Now, eyes closed, she allows herself to revise certain moments: she doesn't get on that bus, doesn't say hello to that man, doesn't go inside that house.

María wishes she had some of the photographs she chose not to bring along when she left for Madrid, now that she's struggling to recall people's faces clearly. She kept one old photo in her suitcase—her with her dad and her sister, in the backyard—and she sometimes becomes absorbed in the way the black and white of the image makes certain marks on the wall behind them stand out. A few months after she got to Madrid, her mother sent a letter she had dictated to Chico: it made her laugh to see the careful handwriting of the first lines, accelerating in the second paragraph, the misshapen calligraphy of "take care." Her mother included one other photograph: in it, one of her nephews was posing in front of a birthday cake, and as Chico smeared Carmen's nose with meringue, her mother sheltered the girl in her lap, cradling her head tenderly. María put it on her bedside table. She guessed that was what they had sent it for. But she put it there as a warning to her aunt: she shouldn't be fooled by her obedience. Sure, she might jump out of bed at dawn, she might cook dinner or clean the bathrooms as soon as she got home from work, but the truth is in the photograph.

When the girl wakes up, María looks into Carmen's eyes: two black pinhead eyes. The baby stretches, María reacts: she sits up at the foot of the bed and cranes her neck to peer into the crib. María has grown used to the way the boy in the house wheedles her, to joking around with the neighbours' daughter; but Carmen, being hers, seems made of different stuff. Carmen shifts as if she wants to sit up: she shakes her legs, just a little at first, kicking when that doesn't work; she waves her arms, casts around for María's eyes. Finally, María stands and goes to the crib, picks up her daughter—that cigarette smell—and gathers her in her arms. Her affection induces no response in the girl. She's not kicking any more, but she extends her little right arm. María thinks Carmen must be pointing to a threadbare stuffed animal in the corner of the bedroom. How proud she feels in that moment: Carmen is clever enough to access her memories and locate herself within them, mature enough to try to show off her toys. Is that it? Is that what's happening, or is María projecting something completely imaginary? Still holding Carmen, María picks up the stuffed animal and hands it to her, but the girl smacks it away: there are no tears, no shrieks, although the baby's movements take on a brusqueness. María takes her little left hand and places it on her chest. "Mummy," she calls herself; "mummy," she repeats, though she knows that to Carmen, she may as well be a stranger. Carmen continues reaching out her right arm, pointing to something María doesn't see.

"What do you want, Carmen?"

Clearly, Carmen understands María's words about as well as María understands Carmen's gestures. Should she let someone know, ask for help? Chico will be working into the evening; María imagines her father lying in bed, her mother sitting at one end of the kitchen table, Soledad sewing at the other. What does her daughter need? The baby extends one arm, she points to a chest of drawers, wide and low to the ground. They've explained to her that the top drawer is Carmen's, the two below that are Chico's, the next two are Soledad's, and at the bottom, they've kept some things that belong to María. There was a time when her space was occupied by some clothing, a notebook, a thick old enamel bracelet she found in the street and wore a few times; the bracelet she threw out, and the rest she packed in her suit-case. But the baby, the baby now: the baby points at the chest of drawers where her mother—María's mother, Carmen's grandmother—changes her nappy every morning.

María realizes her error: it's not affection or attention Carmen wants, it's routine. When Carmen wakes from her nap, she demands that someone pick her up, take her out of the crib, and lie her down on the improvised changing table. It doesn't matter who: her mother's mother, her mother's brother, her mother's sister, or just her actual mother. María is doing it today, but when she goes back to Madrid it could be anyone's job, and Carmen will accept it with the same silence. Carmen isn't afraid of strangers. She's grown accustomed to meeting the night in the arms of women who live on the street, who gather outside the front door. Nor is she afraid of the unfamiliar woman who says "mummy" over and over, and insists on holding her close, offers her a stuffed animal. On the towel, Carmen stops moving around, she lifts her legs a little—the way she does several times every day—and whines because María has skipped some step in the changing. When she considers the girl done, and succeeds in getting the nappy on her, María puts her back in the cot and lies down again on her brother's bed. Before closing her eyes, María has the sensation that Carmen—tiny body stretched out alongside her adult one, both of them searching for sleep—is watching her.

Three or four women at the front door, more later on: eight, maybe nine. Their voices blend together, too similar in tone to tell apart, the same words in different mouths. They gather on the pavement every night; making the pilgrimage with chairs from their neighbouring homes, sometimes sharing food, if husbands won't be getting back until late. The ritual took shape in the early years of the neighbourhood, when María was very small, before her older siblings left home and before the younger ones had been born. In those years, before streetlights, they staved off the night with candles, and the legs of the chairs scraped against dirt. Chico still had the vaguest memory of trips to the spring with their mother. Now the neighbourhood is something else entirely, although the streets still turn into mud when it rains: they've promised to fix that, Chico tells her, he heard as much at the bar a few weeks back. María doesn't feel like much has changed in the last year, but Chico insists there's a lot she wouldn't recognize if she'd go out for a walk with him.

"I'm not even tall enough to reach the bar."

"I find that hard to believe."

María can't help but laugh when Chico explains: he's so short that when he first started working in the bar, the customers didn't even know he was there. Her brother is exaggerating. Reality is always worse in Chico's accounts, or—when happier times come around—better, and María loves the way he describes Soledad's silence, his anecdotes about Carmen, or conversations between the neighbour-hood women.

"The first few days, all they saw was the top of my head, nothing else: a kid's head putting beers down in front of them. Then I made a little platform out of soft-drink crates, now I can get my top half up there."

Chico's nickname won out over his given one. He even introduces himself that way, Chico, just as his father called him the day he was born: the littlest son, a blond baby more bone than flesh, with big blue eyes—like María's—determined not to get any bigger. At age six, he looked more like a four-year-old; now, at thirteen, he could pass for eleven. María had always believed that Chico would be the only one of her siblings who managed to get out of the neighbourhood: he didn't mind school, he liked numbers. She was sorry when she heard that he'd dropped out to work at their older brother's bar. These were her thoughts as she tried to make out her brother's words amid the chattering of the women, five or six or seven of them outside the window. Is she in there? She's in there. In the bedroom, with the girl and her brother. She came? I could never have done it. I couldn't have gone off and left her here, like a piece of rubbish you drop along the way. Well, I wouldn't have gone and done what she did in the first place. Done what? Keep your voices down, her mother will hear. She'll hear. What. Is she coming? Why not Soledad, she's always so quiet, so calm. And the little one. I tried to tell their mother, and she didn't want to listen. Shh, the boy, he's still just a child.

"Don't listen to them," Chico says, confirming María's suspicions. He takes one quick drag after another in front of the crib, Carmen now in María's arms.

"Since when do you smoke?"

"Since I started at the bar. They're always making fun of me. They call me Chica, some of them. I don't like it, but it makes me seem older, don't you think?"

"How much of a nuisance is she?"

"I'm gone all day long. I help Soledad out with her morning jobs in town same as always, but when I get back,

I leave her with whatever's still to do and go to the bar. It's just Toñi and me, but that's fine. We have something to eat, it's usually pretty quiet then, maybe someone comes in for a coffee, then the men playing cards or dominoes, a couple of dinners, and we head home. The kid is almost always asleep. She doesn't have much of a sense of humour, but she's clever. Sometimes I talk to her, and the way she pays attention makes me think she understands. She likes me better than Soledad, that's for sure."

They stop talking, in case their sister hears. More than a link, Soledad represents an ellipsis between the two of them: she was born after María, before Chico, and to both of them, she seems from another planet; she has nothing in common with anyone. She sits in the kitchen, constantly sewing and listening to the radio, and she barely slows down to eat lunch or rest. Sometimes she'll take a break to play some clapping game with Carmen, trying to feign affection, but she quickly gets bored and returns to her work. Chico stubs out his cigarette and reaches for Carmen.

"They left the neighbourhood, María."

"I don't want to know."

"Maybe you don't. But they're gone. You could come back." Chico stops talking, giving María a chance to respond, but his sister is quiet. "What's Madrid like? I'd like to go sometime. Even just to visit."

"There isn't much room at our aunt and uncle's. At first it all felt so strange, I barely knew them... I shared a bed with our cousin the first few months, but since the wedding, I've had the room to myself. I do the same thing as you: wake up and go straight to the bus stop, because the house is a long way away. The family is nice, and they pay me on time. Whatever I cook seems all right with them, and I don't work on Sundays, because they always go out for the day. I'm lucky, that's not how it is for most of the other girls working for families in the building: lots of them sleep there, some work seven days a week. The family has a son who's a little older than Carmen, and he's fussy, but the mother takes care of him. I worry that when he gets a little older, they won't need me any more."

"Well, maybe then you could come back."

"Or take Carmen with me."

She notices Chico looks upset: as if what she suggested would destroy her brother's routine. Carmen shouldn't be up this late, but María allows it because Chico's jokes have provoked the first laugh from the girl all day. The conversation out in the street shows no sign of abating, and María can tell some of the neighbours are still talking about her, what kind of life she must lead out there, there's a reason they sent her away the first chance they had, the baby's better off here.

"Chico, do you miss school?"

"Not any more, but I did at first. I didn't like it at the bar. Think about it. I could have been a teacher. Maybe I'll go back when I'm older, if I leave the bar and have time. I do miss the books they let me borrow, because some nights I get bored. I'll have to come up with some way of passing the time."

Chico is sounding older all of a sudden. María pictures him, hardly thirteen, making sure the neighbour doesn't leave without paying his tab, giving orders to his sister-in-law, behind the bar eating leftovers from the day's special, cigarette dangling from his mouth. She thinks of the smile Chico keeps up in front of them all, but also of what Chico must think about every night, in his little bed, while the baby sleeps and tight-lipped Soledad goes on sewing.

"At night she cries like you wouldn't believe. Remember the first few months? Well, it's the complete opposite. It doesn't matter if you're having the best dream of your life, she'll knock you right out of it screaming. Soledad just pulls her pillow over her head, so I always have to deal with it. Do babies have nightmares?"

She was only there for a short time after Carmen was born; what she knows comes from phone calls or the odd letter, or the times when her employer goes out for a walk and leaves the boy behind, and that's how María found out about the sweet scent, so different from her daughter's. The baby smells like cigarettes, just like Chico, whose nails are turning yellow from the nicotine. The street confabulations don't stop, and even now, at the edge of sleep—everything just as it was right after she'd given birth: Carmen in the crib, she and her brother in the little bed, and in the other bed, sound asleep, Soledad—she can hear the neighbours talking about her. Sometimes she makes out her mother's voice, avoiding getting drawn into it or attempting to change the subject. They left the neighbourhood, María hears one of the women say. The wife found out. How could anyone stick around and see her every day, on the same street, with his eyes. They had to at least do that. María feels Chico's slender form move away from hers, and her brother gets up to close the window.

"It's chilly in here," he says. "We can't let the baby catch cold."

She hears Chico rummage around in his drawer and leave the room. Soledad carefully opens the door, puts her pyjamas on in the dark, says goodnight; the mattress creaks under the weight of her body. Silence: the neighbours are going home, chair legs scraping the pavement as they leave. Chico gets into bed and turns his back to hers, so he's facing the wall. Her brother smells like cigarettes, María thinks, and moments later Carmen wakes up crying.

María starts to tell it to herself, silently moving her lips, her daughter and siblings asleep in the room: she senses the heat from Chico's back, the engine in her daughter's chest, Soledad's deep breathing. There's so much I want to say, but I can't get it in the right order. She does the same as on other nights: rehearsing the words she'll say to her mother, the words she'll say to Carmen once she can understand. She takes the situations she's lived through back up again, start to finish, even the ones that don't seem important; she corrects a few gestures and almost all of the decisions, she supplies them with happy endings out of step with reality. Carmen, for example: in the stories María thinks up before going to sleep, Carmen doesn't exist. María's never heard the father's voice, she's never seen a grey city, or she'll only see one on holiday years later. But Carmen does exist, her cry breaks open the night, and she wakes up María and Chico and Soledad who—as María was forewarned—hides her head under the pillow, pretending she's asleep. Carmen exists, and sometimes her eyes are like insects she'd stomp on, and at other times like little dots she'd play at connecting into a shape, and it occurs to María that maybe she could bring her back to the city and ask her aunt to keep an eye on her while she works. María, to herself: I want to say so many things, but I don't know how to get them in order. They're in my head, I think them all the time, but they disappear before I can put them into words. I understand that I made a mistake, that I was reckless, that I brought shame on myself, and on all of you. If I weren't sending money here, if I kept it all, maybe I could give a little more to my aunt and uncle, save the rest, and at some point Carmen and I could live together. Just ask my aunt and uncle, they'll tell you: I never go out except on some Sundays with my cousin and her husband, and I always come straight home from work. Carmen doesn't know who I am, and I have no way of describing her to people. When they ask what she looks like, what faces she makes, I tell them about the portrait I keep on my bedside table. My daughter doesn't move, she doesn't talk, she doesn't know who I am. She's locked up in a photograph.

She doesn't talk to her mother. None of them talk to their mother, really, nor to their father: each one plays a role, never deviating from the others' expectations. The parents act like parents, they make plans and give orders, and the children act like children, they obey; María's mistake was defying that logic. Since she returned, her mother has limited conversation to sharing details about Carmen—don't worry about that noise, we've figured out it's not that she's tired, or hungry, or hurting: she just likes to hear herself, that's all—and complaining that Chico wastes his time at the bar then forgets to bring ice back for the fridge, or that her father sleeps too late. As soon as she arrived, she stuck her head in his room and said hello, went over to kiss his forehead. She wanted to ask him something, how things were going, to tell him about his brother—the one she lives with in Madrid, he'd said to send his regards—but Soledad called her back to the kitchen, and as María went out, her father asked her to shut the door.

Some dead leaves have appeared in the flowerpots in the backyard: María thinks her mother must not be tall enough to water them all, and they're in direct sunlight. Sometimes she and Soledad would take out the chairs when the weather was good, and sit and sew, the clothing in their laps, so it didn't get dirty, careful not to drop needles or thread on the ground. On one visit to the workshop, she had seen the sewing machines—the women operating them, quickly, quickly—the noise they made like a battle, but when she and her sister worked, there was nothing but the sharp intake of breath from Soledad pricking her finger, or an argument drifting over from a neighbouring yard. When they dropped something—a dress slipping from their hands onto the tiny gravel stones, or worse: a needle going missing between them—the two of them sat bolt upright as though the fabric, copper, or metal had hit them. Sometimes it was María cursing her own clumsiness, and then Soledad would scold her, but when it was Soledad's doing, she just fell silent. How many black and white threads, how many blue or green ones, had already disappeared in the gravel? How many pins? Carmen would play in the yard one day, and María foresaw her daughter's future tantrum, after one of them pricked her bottom or the palm of her hand.

When the family moved into the house, María's father roughed out a path to the toilet with large white stones—it was to go across the entire backyard so you could avoid walking in the dirt, which sometimes turned to mud, but he never actually filled it in. Her older brothers, who were bricklayers, told her they'd gone on to finish the job themselves, taking materials here and there from the other houses they were working on, some of which had cement paths, others tiled ones, the result being a clumsy mishmash. The solution at their parents' house had more to do with carelessness than modesty: a few neighbours had asked her mother why she didn't plant some fruit trees, as they had, instead of the flowerpots scattered against the dirty white wall, some hanging at the height of the sons who no longer lived there. María never heard her mother's reply—silence, some evasive comment, *better that than nothing*—but she did hear what she said behind closed doors, her satisfaction when the roots buckled the most ambitious neighbours' cement paths, and they had to remove the trees and pay for repairs; her mother's glee when the wasps made their rounds through the grapevines in the other backyards, destroying the fruit, the odour of garlic compresses for the pain of their stings wafting all the way to their house. I wouldn't mind if they kept them up all night, she said through clenched teeth, I wouldn't mind if they never got a decent night's sleep again. But wasps can't see in the dark, Chico said, it doesn't matter what those women plant in their yards, it'll only be a problem during the day. María heard her mother's laughter go flat.

Chico insists that the neighbourhood has changed completely, and in the time it took for María to walk from the bus stop in the town centre to the door of their house—no one met her to help with her suitcase—she thought her brother was exaggerating. But when she walks to the square with Carmen, she realizes he's right, though for different reasons: in casting her mind back to what these streets were like, she's placing them alongside the ones where she lives now. She substitutes a gridded design—exact parallels, exact perpendiculars—for one of another sort: stones here, dirt there; they do, in fact, make their way diagonally to a centre. María notices while she's retracing the path of their beloved Saturday- or Sunday-morning walks, hers and Soledad's and Chico's, like this: the girls arm in arm, and him going on ahead. Now she holds Carmen against her chest, in her arms, facing outwards, and if the weight gets to be too much, she shifts her to one hip; in the doorway of one of the houses, a girl the same age plays with two boys, one a little older than Carmen, the other a little younger. The church where the neighbourhood association meets is in the square; the next-door neighbour's daughter takes typing classes there, they ran into each other the moment she stepped outside the house, the girl called her Madrileña. "Madrileña!" she said, just a few years older than Chico, and asked if she'd met any famous artists in the capital yet. María said no, that all she does is work, and the girl was disappointed she'd moved to a whole other city just for that. As they were walking away, Carmen looked at María and brought her little fist up and hit her on the chin, possibly in agreement with the girl.

In her aunt and uncle's neighbourhood, in Madrid, the cars—the few there are—don't get stuck in the mud, they go from place to place and crash into each other and speed along on cobblestone roads. The girls her age look like her and Soledad, and the parents look like their parents; she hears accents like her own. Even so, while she's just like the girl from the typing class, or the one who's keeping her children entertained on the pavement outside their house, she feels different: luckier than Chico or Carmen, even. She thinks about Soledad. How much time will she have to spend sewing in that kitchen, walking to the square alone on weekends for a breath of fresh air? There's not enough room in the high school she and her siblings went to for all the kids born in the neighbourhood now. Will that be Carmen's fate? Will Chico teach her reading and maths at night, sitting in bed so they don't wake the grandparents? On those streets she hardly recognizes, a house and a shop and a bar, one house, another, another, all of them the same, María strolls along with Carmen, not, though, serenely enjoying this window of time with her daughter before heading home, but rather hoping to cross paths with someone she knows, hoping to hear her name called out by some acquaintance, to be asked, How are you? She doesn't recognize anyone: she's forgotten the faces, the names. The houses run out and there's nothing left but countryside, more land, whatever else is out there. She asks a woman how to get home. Your home? Where do you live?

María places a towel on the chest of drawers and lies the girl down on top of it: she smells of shit, of course, and she can tell from the way the cloth feels that she must have also wet herself on the walk. The boy at the house where she works, he'll certainly let you know, he hates a damp nappy, but Carmen doesn't make a peep, just waiting until someone realizes it's there, that time has passed. Legs up, María orders, lifting her little dress, undoing the nappy, which has a bit of diarrhoea in it; she'll ask her mother if that's a frequent occurrence, and if not, make a mental note of what Carmen ate. Hands in the hot water, she rubs the bar of soap between them and gives the dirty bottom a clean. She pats her dry with the towel, the wash mitt comes off, then a fine layer of talcum powder to cover her skin. Legs up, and then she says her name: legs up, Carmen. Help me out, will you? That's it. The girl raises her legs and María takes hold of her by the ankles; unmindful of her own strength, she lifts the baby's entire body, trying to get it up just enough to slide the nappy between the surface and her bum, but the girl protests. She whimpers softly at first, then the crying comes, the full fanfare. Soledad asks what's happened, her father, too; her mother, off chatting on the doorstep of some neighbour or another, doesn't hear. Soledad leaves before María can respond, scolding her for not lending a hand with the sewing, for all that she's deigned to come and visit. What happened is, the baby is a baby, and she cries. María drops her ankles unthinkingly, not accounting for her legs hitting the wooden top; with all the noise, she barely registers the dull thud of her delicate flesh. The girl is still whimpering on the chest of drawers; maybe it's the hard surface that's bothering her, so María picks her up and moves the big towel over to Chico's bed. She struggles to lay it out then sets

Carmen down on top of it. Legs up, Carmen: please. Legs up, and keep them there. The girl isn't whining any more, but her face is all tears and snot, and her lips are trembling. Carmen, please, don't make this difficult. Carmen doesn't budge, so María tries to sneak the cloth under her body: it works. It gets dark too fast—every manoeuvre takes minutes and minutes—and she can hardly tell any more where to tie one knot or the other. A hand moves hers aside: Chico, you're back early.

"Yeah, Toñi let me go early. I told him you're leaving first thing."

María collapses onto the mattress, the side Carmen has left unoccupied. She watches the way her brother handles the baby, notices where his gestures differ from hers. Chico treats Carmen like a toy: he holds her wrists and brings her palms together in applause, sings to her while he tries to get her to blow her nose into a handkerchief. Chico sees her watching and explains: you treat her like you're afraid of her, and she can sense it. Carmen sniffles, opens her arms, and closes them around Chico. María hears her speak a word: no one told her Carmen was talking. Carmen hangs on to Chico, and María leans in to listen. Her speaking a word, does she know who María is? Carmen's head on Chico's shoulder, Carmen calling him Mummy.

THE KINGDOM

Córdoba, 1998

W HAT HAPPENED THE DAY before the nightmare that replays for Alicia every night? She woke up to her mother's nagging, reluctantly dressed for school—jeans, sandals, a T-shirt bearing the logo of some sports brand— she came home. It wasn't long till summer holidays, till the move, till she'd be starting secondary school. Many bodies intersect with that story: her tiny mother; her tiny sister; her father, with his broad shoulders; the almost-teenagers walking the playground at break time. She doesn't remember their faces, hardly remembers a name. Their bodies don't show up in the nightmare Alicia has every night. Her father's body does. Is that him crashing into the tree, limping along before hanging himself, or is she just recreating herself in her father's image? To understand what her father felt that day, before he made up his mind—before he chose a quiet road, accelerated into a curve, misjudged it and veered into the hillside, somehow still missing the cliff edge, limped along, and, finally, hanged himself—Alicia often finds herself going over his facial expressions, his words, one by one.

———

From the middle of the living room, she could look out at the street without being seen by anyone. It happened in that house, in that enormous room: the biggest room Alicia had ever been in. If she leant out over the balcony, they would of course catch sight of her easily, behind her mother's flowerpots, her red scrunchie, her fair hair. But positioning herself in the middle of the living room, she could see anyone crossing over to the square before they got to her building; she could stay one step ahead, look into her future.

When the clock read 5 p.m., she stood in that precise spot, under the ceiling light. She'd agreed with her classmates that they wouldn't arrive before then, and she was banking on them being slightly later since Celia was never on time: she lived a long way away, on the outskirts of the neighbourhood near the Madrid road, and she wasn't good at calculating distances. Even so, when the time came, Alicia stood up from the sofa, turned off the TV, and kept watch. Ten minutes later, Inma appeared, and shortly after, Celia, jogging along—she paused before crossing the street, leaning against a lamp post to catch her breath. They exchanged a few words, then came towards Alicia's house. A few minutes later, the buzzer rang.

Why did Alicia choose to do that project with Inma and Celia? They were told to work in groups of three, the two of them were always together, and Alicia hadn't been able to join any other group. She went over to Celia, who sat two desks down and received the proposal with resignation, maybe distrust; Inma, on the other hand, responded enthusiastically. In that moment, on that day, neither reaction seemed like a problem to Alicia; it was problem solved, as far as she was concerned. But the next morning, Celia explained that her house was too full up with people for them to meet there, and Inma said hers wouldn't work either; her grandmother was sick and needed quiet. So Alicia, who had avoided saying any more about herself than was necessary, had to open her immense living room to those nobodies.

But no, Alicia wasn't being truthful: it was actually Celia's efforts to protect Inma she was interested in. Innocent, trusting Inma, the butt of every joke, her cheeks burning at the slightest comment; and Celia, ready to lash out at anyone who made fun of her friend, her devotion more the kind you'd expect from a mother than an older sister or a best friend. To this day Alicia still thinks of Celia, trying to recover her breath after racing to be on time, of her hips, widened into a woman's too early; she wonders how her life turned out: if she and Inma are still friends, if she already has three or four children, if their lives are at all alike. Alicia remembers that Celia liked to draw, that she populated the margins of her textbooks with delicate flowers, and that she hid coloured pencils in her lap and shaded in those gardens between language or history lessons. About Inma, there wasn't much more she could say. She always wore her hair in a braid, talked about her grandmother and her older brother constantly.

It wasn't the first time Inma and Celia had peered into the large window of Alicia's house: since she arrived at class in September, almost every group of girls had made their way to the square at some point, and stopped—arm in arm—before the building. The same faces turned up again term after term, so that anyone new—someone who'd been held back a year, someone whose family had moved in—brought with them a mysterious legend. For Hashim, they invented a troubled past, an orphanage straight out of the movies, when actually he lived with his parents and siblings in the new apartment complex across from the shopping centre. Yoli, who'd had to repeat several years, had struggled with her studies because her dad ran off with a woman from his office. They never did find out if that was the case, because Yoli's mother, and Yoli and her two little brothers, twins, redheads just like her, left the city at the end of the school year. In the movies they screened outside during the summer, the kids and their parents would build tree houses, then the kids would climb up strips of wood nailed into the trunk and hide there, far away from the adults. Inma, Celia, Marta, Rosi: their forest the four spindly trees in the park, the yellow dirt, the metal swings, scorching to the touch in June. Their tree house was the stories they made up about their classmates.

They hadn't yet perfected a story for Alicia. Everything about her threw them: her handwriting was flawless, she remembered dates and the names of historic figures, didn't yawn in class. They couldn't understand why she'd been held back, but what really confused them had nothing to do with her mental aptitude: she had different pairs of shoes for each day of the week, she took care to show off the brand of her jeans. That's how Alicia piqued their curiosity: when she sat down, she pulled her shirt up to her waistband; at break time, complained that her new Nikes were giving her blisters. Celia thought about the clothes her mother bought at the second-hand shop on the boulevard; about her trousers, the same trousers everyone else was wearing, their fake labels with one letter changed so they looked like the in-fashion ones: Zappa rather than Kappa, Pila rather than Fila. Inma never even got any of those new: all her clothes were hand-me-downs from her cousin.

It wasn't the first time Inma and Celia, Celia and Inma, together since crèche, had stopped at the crossing in front of Alicia's building and strained to see something—the silhouette of her mother bringing her a snack, the sofa where her father would sit—through the window. They never had any luck: they got tired of waiting for something, real or imagined, to explode, and changed their route. They knew Alicia had a younger sister, Eva, and that next year both of them would be transferring to the Carmelite school because their parents had bought an apartment in the nice part of the neighbourhood, in one of the buildings with a garage and a pool. At break they watched Eva choreograph dances for her friends, making up steps for hit songs. Alicia's mother didn't work, or she worked at home, but they'd also heard a woman went there to clean sometimes, because Alicia would mention it: I can't work on the project this afternoon because our girl is coming, our girl moves our schoolwork off the shelf to dust.

The buzzer sounds: they're even smaller in Alicia's memory, Inma a porcelain figurine to put on display in the living-room cabinet, Celia with her little girl's body, one more in line with her age. The buzzer sounds, then Alicia's mother grumbling in her bedroom, trying to stay asleep, and her sister's intense excitement at having visitors. Alicia stood behind the door, waiting for the *click* of the lift arriving at the fourth floor, then opened it for them before Celia could buzz again.

"My mother's having her siesta."

It amused Alicia—or does it amuse her now, years later, closer in circumstances to those girls than the adult she was supposed to have become—how careful they'd been with their outfits. Celia had on the same jeans she'd been wearing earlier, but she had changed her T-shirt, which advertised an awning company, for a white sleeveless blouse with lace trim, maybe taken from her mother's chest of drawers. A summer dress had been chosen for Inma, chequered, with straps; the top part was tight as anything on her, and she had to keep readjusting it just to move. Alicia's sister looked at them, smiling, while Alicia merely went and sat down at the big table, waiting for them to join her in gluing cut-outs onto the poster.

"We'll show you around the apartment," her sister announced, taking Inma by the hand.

She assumed the role of hostess and made her way up the hall. While Alicia had been standing in the middle of the room, trying to glimpse the visitors before the intercom buzzed, it seemed her sister had been planning her approach, imagining how she'd entertain these two strangers. Her sister—four years younger than Alicia, with a face full of freckles and a couple of gaps in her smile, thanks to her clumsiness—was opening the door to the bathroom, pointing to the toilet and the washing machine, the threadbare towels. She led Celia and Inma around, proudly showed off her bedroom: an

entire room just for her, painted pink, with her name spelt
out in big letters in the middle of the bookshelf; the stuffed
animals, the dolls, some children's books, a little TV for when
she woke up early on weekends and wanted to entertain
herself without bothering anyone. She left her room and
opened the door to Alicia's, pointing out another TV—a
little bigger than hers, their parents had observed a certain
hierarchy—the shelving with her collection of miniatures,
some dolls covered in dust. She resisted her urge to show
them the closet, but Alicia saw Celia admiring her trainers.
The little girl let go of Inma's hand and started pulling Celia
along instead. They passed their parents' bedroom—there
they would have found Alicia's mother, eyes closed, listening to the commotion in the hallway, and another TV, and
a chest of drawers that spanned the entire wall, and high
heels scattered across the floor like breadcrumbs to mark the
way back home—and went into their father's office, with
the desktop computer and modem. Inma asked if they had
internet, and Alicia's sister said yes, incapable of imagining
that the girls didn't use Yahoo to look up the answers for
their homework assignments.

"But if someone calls, it stops working," she complained.

They still had the master bathroom, the bidet, the tub, the
immense mirror where their father shaved and their mother
applied her make-up, where Alicia and her sister leant in to
complete the family portrait. The creams, the perfumes: not
the family-sized bottle of baby cologne Inma's mother sprayed
her daughter with every day, but delicate glass bottles—a
few drops behind your ear, along your neckline—which
their father had given their mother, just because. They still

had the kitchen, the microwave, the double-door fridge, the empty bags from El Corte Inglés in a careless heap. Alicia didn't know where she'd gotten her extremely keen sense of smell—not from her mother, not from her father—but on Celia she could detect the odour of newly peeled potatoes, more plant than food.

Alicia, her sister Eva, Inma and Celia: the four returned to the living room, Alicia going straight to the table to lay out the poster paper and pass around glue sticks, Eva intent on showing them the terrace. Some flowerpots their mother watered with care—Alicia never learnt the names of the plants—a pair of chairs where she would sunbathe in her bikini. Inma and Eva went out to conclude the tour; Celia stayed in the living room, just where Alicia had stood a little earlier, under the chandelier. Celia didn't seem to care about the exterior, Alicia thought, didn't care what was happening outside, in the world she knew by heart. She stared at the TV screen that took up half the console, the VCR their father had recently bought, the stereo equipment, the collection of movies and CDs, and the photos from all their family holidays: Alicia in one frame, dancing with other girls at a hotel in Marbella; Alicia and Eva and their parents in another, smiling at Disneyland Paris: Eva in a hat with ears, Sleeping Beauty's tower coming out of their father's head, Celia's pupils so dilated that her green eyes were tinted black.

From time to time, Inma and Celia also went back to that afternoon at Alicia's apartment. In the weeks that followed, they had a hard time explaining to the others what had happened. Everyone asked if they had gone inside, if they'd been shown around, if they were there when the phone rang the first time, or for that second call. Inma answered at first—yes, there was a TV in every room; yes, we drank fizzy drinks; no, we didn't leave right away—and Celia was silent. She didn't say a word even when her parents told her some rumour they'd heard in the downstairs bar, in a clumsy attempt to make their daughter feel less alone. Years later, Celia began to add in certain details: one day, at school, between classes, the pink quilt in Eva's room came back to her; later, on an Erasmus year in Coimbra, she sent Inma a long email in which she described the feelings that came up for her when she thought of that afternoon, being so close to all those luxuries, unthinkable for two girls like them. For the first time, she spoke of the envy she'd felt towards Alicia that whole year, those expensive tracksuits versus the outfits they had to be content with, and for the first time, she also mentioned her relief that afternoon—at the end of that afternoon—the comfort of going home, seeing her mother and aunt on the sofa, her little brother and her two cousins finishing their homework, her grandmother in the rocking chair, the blinds lowered, hastening the night's arrival. The comfort, too, of hearing the door close when her aunt and her cousins left, and the comfort later on, hearing it open again when her father got in from work: she ran to hug him, and her father stained her shirt with grease from the workshop. Celia added a subject line that was seemingly unrelated: "The Wonders."

Inma read it straight away but took several weeks to respond. She typed and deleted, rewrote until she'd distilled a paragraph to two sentences; the next day, she picked it back up again. In the end, she was able to tell Celia that for years she had felt that what happened that afternoon was divine retribution: greed is a cardinal sin, or at least that's what her grandmother had taught her. What did one family need all that for, those TVs, those holidays; she wondered about it every night, turning it over in her mind like a refrain. She didn't know what had bothered her more: the innocent way Eva led them around the house, oblivious as she showed off their standard of living, or Alicia's indifference at receiving them, her total lack of interest in sharing any of her private life. Celia answered immediately, firing off an email of just a few lines, some anecdote about a party the night before.

They didn't forget Alicia or Eva: not even Carmen, their mother, barely a body, asleep and breathing on the other side of the door, barely a voice, rising from stammer to shout. Over the years, Celia and Inma—Inma and Celia—would recall that afternoon from time to time, leaving the cinema, helping with a move, or on a visit to the hospital, one of their children newly born.

"Do you think we're going to turn into them?" one or the other would ask.

And one or the other would grimace and say no, doing an imitation laugh that contained both desire and terror.

Alicia's memories of that day are not in chronological order. Discrete scenes: for example, she's unable to reconstruct the moments after her alarm clock went off but before she came back home from school: hours—she can't even say how many—during which she stretches and gets out of bed, their mother shouts for her to hurry up and shower, her sister spills chocolate milk on her pinafore, their mother shouts at her to help Eva change. Eva, however, maintained in the few short years before Alicia left for Madrid that although their father usually got up before them and ate breakfast out, on that day he'd decided to take them to school; she spilt her milk, yes, but he went to her room with her, and together they picked out another dress for her to wear to school. In both stories—Alicia's and Eva's—the mother isn't up, or rather, she's still in bed: she used to give out instructions from under the covers, what they should do, how to do it, interspersed with the occasional yawn. After that, Alicia gets lost. She walked to school with Eva, or with Eva and their father, went inside the older years' building after getting her sister to her own classroom, or she kissed her father's cheek so she could walk the last few metres alone, without anyone seeing that he'd been with her. She sat through three lessons; at break time, went and told Celia and Inma when to come over that afternoon; her teacher from the previous year applauded her progress. After the three remaining subjects—religion or art, maybe, who knows—she put her books and notebooks inside her backpack, said goodbye to Celia, ran to get her sister. Hold on, now: Alicia thinks her sister is waiting over by the gate, in an orange dress, the fabric very soft—the kind her mother never would have let her get dirty playing on the playground. Yes: dirt stains on her sister's dress, as if she'd thrown herself to the ground, imitating some dance move. Yes: maybe her sister was right, maybe her father had decided to stay home longer than usual that day, in anticipation of what was going to happen later on. Alicia grabbed her sister's hand—she has forgotten the way it felt to hold her father's—and they went home. They ate lunch—what did they eat: almost twenty years, and still there's that knot in her stomach—her sister shut herself up in her bedroom to watch TV, her mother in hers for her siesta, Alicia watched a show and, at five o' clock, turned the TV off, took up position at the centre of the living room, directly beneath the ceiling light, and waited for her classmates to arrive.

"Do you want fizzy drinks?"

"I'm not allowed. My mummy says it gives you cancer."

"My aunt puts it on her skin when she sunbathes, she says it makes her tan faster. You drink it? Is it nice?"

"Yeah, I like it. My mum's taking a nap. How about yours?"

"Mine's at home."

"Mine's at the supermarket."

"She's out running errands or something?"

"No, that's where she works."

While Inma carefully cut out little shapes, Celia transcribed some of the texts they wanted to include on poster paper of another colour, and Alicia wrote out the title at the top of the poster. Her sister had brought out some colouring books meant for younger children, which she still enjoyed. Eva offered them sweets and refreshments, she asked about relatives she'd never so much as met; mimicked their mother's demeanour, that same insistent prattling, more noise than conversation.

"Eva, shut up and leave us alone, we're studying."

She went quiet, and when Inma asked what year she was in, what subjects she liked, what she wanted to be when she grew up, the girl barely offered monosyllables. As on other occasions when Eva had turned into a shrunken version of their mother, Alicia had managed to deactivate her, had returned her to her natural state: a nine-year-old girl incapable of adjusting her tone, or of anything more than navel-gazing.

Inma's mother works at a supermarket; Celia's, wherever she can. Some months she mops stairs, others she helps out at a salon; Celia once said something in class that made Alicia think she'd even worked at one of her father's restaurants for a while. If Alicia believed in dreams and prophesies, she would explain that, on that day, her future had been revealed to her at a big table in the living room of her home, in front of a poster she'd been assigned to make for natural sciences. But that doesn't happen: she believes in little now—then, even less—and on that afternoon, she just felt like having fun. In a few days, she would be saying goodbye to them forever—Alicia didn't think families like theirs could afford the tuition at her new school—and there was nothing about them she could bring herself to like; they were ridiculous, in their Sunday best on a weekday.

"Inma, do you have internet at home?"

"We don't have a computer."

"But have you ever logged on to the internet?"

"No. Once in the library, I think it was Vicky. I think Vicky was the one who did it."

"It was really slow," Celia added. "Vicky knows how because her neighbours have it."

"Do you guys have TVs?"

"Yeah, we do."

"Yeah, in the living room."

"But just in the living room, right?"

"In the living room, yeah."

"Same for us, just in the living room. But we don't have it on very much, because my grandma's sick."

"We do, all the time. When my aunt comes over, it's on the whole time."

"Here, we can watch whatever we want in our rooms."

Eva was colouring a shape, trying to stay inside the lines. Alicia, thinking about what to say next, admired her effort not to leave a single patch of white, but also not to go beyond the edges of the drawing. Alicia channelled that same care and attention into searching for words that would hurt Celia and Inma. This is something both she and the girls will remember, but for them the memory will be streaked with shame.

"And your outfits today, Inma, Celia… I *love* them."

"Thanks. This dress is new."

"Oh? Where did you get it? I'd love to have something like that."

"I got it last week. My cousin's grown out of it already, around the chest. She's very mature. But she only wore it two or three times. So really, it's almost new."

"From the flea market, maybe?"

"No, I don't think so. My cousin goes to the shops in the neighbourhood, she doesn't go all the way out there."

"Where is the flea market, Celia? I've never been."

When Alicia said "Celia," she looked up to meet her eyes. First, she saw Eva, concentrating hard, her tongue at the corner of her mouth, then Inma, who was focused on the landscape she was trying to cut out; then, finally, Celia. Celia had put the cap back on the pen and crossed her arms, she had worked out what she was up to, her burning eyes already on Alicia. That's when Alicia realized her mistake—she should have known better. Sure, she could make fun of Inma; to Inma, her spite would seem like curiosity, she'd be flattered that Alicia wanted to know more about her life, might even imagine, in those few minutes of conversation, a friendship: summer afternoons in front of the TV, in front of the air conditioner. But that's not how it would go with Celia: she felt every attack on Inma, was enraged by every attack on her. One word could be enough for her to tear into Alicia, who had witnessed her reactions in the hallways at school: the day they came close to expelling her, when Dani lifted up Inma's skirt, and Celia had grabbed him by the neck; Dani's feet centimetres off the ground, Inma's fists clenched, the same exact expression on Celia's face.

"The flea market is over by the church, in the car park near the main road. On Tuesdays and Fridays. I don't go because I'm in class, but my mum sometimes does when she's not working, just for something to do. These jeans are from the flea market, and the shirt is from the new second-hand shop, over by the first bar your dad opened. Your mum's uncle lives over there, right? I think one of my neighbours knows him."

Alicia was confused, in that moment, by Celia's response; she'd been hoping for a scene—for her to uncross her arms and hit her, for Eva to yell and her mother to burst in. The next day they would have talked about it in class, and the teacher might have even called in Celia's parents, and Inma's parents, and Alicia's parents, to find some way of moving forward, with the end of the school year just a few days away. But Celia stopped talking and went back to work, hurrying now, trying to finish copying out her portion of the text as quickly as possible. To Alicia, Celia seemed clever; clever and, with her brisk reply, direct. She regretted having spent a whole year in her class and hardly having spoken to her; she also regretted underestimating her, hurting her. No, actually: in that moment, Alicia was enjoying the situation, Inma deceived by her flattery and Celia humiliated, without internet or TVs, and in that ridiculous shirt with its lace trim. Alicia can't pretend that at thirteen she felt the remorse she feels in her thirties, nor can she imagine, as a teenager, the empathy she's still missing, even today.

Then the phone rang.

A real preoccupation of Celia's, in her work as a teacher, was detecting students who awoke in her the image of that afternoon. She had identified an "Alicia type," she told Inma. A girl who thought herself superior in some way because she'd grown up with money, because she knew she was more attractive or more intelligent than the others, and who tried to surround herself with girls who were less well off, who were duller or plainer. That old swimming-pool trick: when you climb up on someone else's shoulders and jump, launching yourself while at the same time sinking them. A few weeks into each year, she and Inma would call each other up to analyse their students: at first with beginners' enthusiasm, then with the boredom that comes with learning a lesson by heart. Celia insisted that Inma noticed it less because in the

56

sciences it was harder to break through to the humanity of the students, but in art history, the subject matter facilitated precisely that: an Alicia, Celia explained, an Alicia never lets emotion in. An Alicia pretends to let emotion in; she goes all wide-eyed because she knows that's her role, that's what's expected of her. That girl had become an archetype for them. Over the years, as they shed their weaknesses and their goodness, Inma and Celia—Celia and Inma—would recall her like an after-dinner anecdote. As time passed, they'd become an audience of two: they occupied their two chairs at the living-room table, heard the telephone ring, heard Carmen's words and Eva's sobbing, what could have happened to Carmen, what could have happened to Eva; Alicia's silence. But time placed them at a distance, pushed them out of the scene; first, Celia and Inma sat on the balcony and watched the goings-on inside; later on, they had been ejected onto the street, back to that pedestrian crossing where they had stood and stared in at the big picture window.

"Then the phone rang," Celia would always say in closing. "It's absurd, isn't it? For that to be the way their lives changed, forever. With a phone call."

Then the phone rang. Alicia's mother picked up, as always: the phone rang in the living room and her bedroom. Alicia didn't understand why she then burst in as she did, in front of the girls; it unsettled her that her mother, who insisted on a full face of make-up even just for her daughters, would allow two strangers to see her veiny legs, the purple spiderwebs around her knee. The phone rang and Alicia caught a few of her mother's words, her saying, No, that they kept the account book in the office. The noises that followed, however, didn't send her in the direction of the office, but to the room where the girls were: her mother burst in, located a black notebook on the shelf, next to the TV, paying no attention to Celia or Inma and picking up the other phone.

"I'm here, he had it somewhere else. I just remembered that last night, while we were watching TV, he wrote something down, and he left it out here. I'll give you the number now."

Her mother's voice put a stop to the screeching of markers against poster paper. Eva was no longer colouring in, neither was Alicia; Inma dropped the scissors on the table, and Celia put the cap back on her pen. The friends looked at each other, paying close attention to the conversation, trying to guess at the voice on the other end, who it was, what they were saying.

Then the phone rang, and that woman came into the living room like a ghost: the black slip against very pale skin, the straps black, the lace black and the skin so, so pale, circles under her eyes from the mascara running. The phone rang, and neither Alicia nor Eva went to pick it up: Celia and Inma could just make out the mother's voice in the distance, much further away than the hallway. The girls put their tasks aside to listen, making no effort to hide it: no marker tips against the thick poster paper, no scissor edge on the outline of a mountain. Carmen spoke haltingly while she located an address—Inma was sure of it—or a phone number—Celia was sure of it—rattled something off, and thanked whomever it was she was talking to for their efforts.

"I don't know, he's usually gone before I get up. He told me last night that today he was planning to check in on all the restaurants… I was thinking he'd eat at the one in town because we were with my uncle the day before yesterday. You're telling me nobody's seen him all day, not once. And you've called everywhere. No, no, I don't doubt it, I'm just asking, that's all. Can you put my uncle on the phone, please? OK, then tell him to call me as soon as he gets to one, tell everybody he needs to call me, wherever he is. It's not that I'm worried, but you have to understand, this is very unusual. I'm not worried. Please don't talk to me like I'm an idiot. Look, I'll call a taxi and go down there myself. Tell everyone that my uncle is to meet me there as soon as he's done. Don't call here again, I'm on my way."

Carmen vanished from the living room as abruptly as she had appeared before Celia and Inma: a presence burst forth from some unknown place. Carmen, for Celia and for Inma, had turned into someone not of this world.

What Alicia does remember is that, on that afternoon, her mother called her to her bedroom as she was getting dressed to leave, and said:

"Alicia, your father has disappeared. He hasn't been to a single restaurant all morning, he's not at the office or the new apartment. He's not answering his phone, and now, the calls don't even seem to be going through. His secretary called the hospitals and the police, but no one knows anything. Uncle Chico is out looking for him, he's stopping at every restaurant to let everyone know he's missing. Tell your friends to go home, please."

But what her mother really said that afternoon when she called Alicia to her bedroom, as she was getting dressed to leave, was:

"They can't find your father, Ali. I'm going to the restaurant in town, to see if I can work out what's going on. Look after Eva, please, and don't mention anything to her. I'm going to ask Aunt Soledad to come keep an eye on you, let's see if I have time before I call the taxi… Only open the door for her, no one else; she doesn't have keys. Or for your father if he comes back, of course. Your friends can stay if you want them here, you can keep each other busy. Not a word about this to Eva. Put on cartoons for her, will you? I don't want her getting scared."

A family left the city and drove up into the hills for a picnic, taking advantage of the pleasant breeze. In the distance, the youngest daughter saw the body of a man. The girl was thrilled by the discovery: it was just like the drawings she did for fun, the figure's head attached to the rope, the rope hanging from a branch, the blank spaces below feet that would never again tread the earth. The mother screamed, the father wondered whether to put his foot down and forget all about it or stop. He parked a few metres away—a car smashed against a tree, the hanged man's car; by some miracle it hadn't caught fire—and approached carefully, as if death were catching. The dead man had closed his eyes when he jumped, and the blood that had run from his nostrils and mouth had dried in the heat. The living man went back to his car, drove to the nearest petrol station at the foot of the hill, and from there called the police.

The first few days, the talk in the neighbourhood was of an accident: the family had been thinking of moving to a house in the country, the new apartment had turned out to be too small before they'd even moved their things in, or the dead man had been looking to expand the business by acquiring a steak house out of town—and had been in such a hurry getting back from wherever it was that he lost control of the car. Someone—the living man, some employee, maybe the police who took the body away—described the noose as being put together with safety belts, the car smashed into the tree in an attempt to simulate an accident; word spread to the neighbourhood bars, lowered voices in the kitchens of his restaurants. People asked Inma and Celia if they'd heard anything unusual in that house. Inma would make some comment, Celia was always silent; a legend was built around them—that they were there to hear Carmen's desperate cry when she answered the phone, or when they told her that her husband was dead. For months, close friends of the couple would surface, accomplices to their beach getaways, people who attested to infidelities, some who even insisted the dead man appeared in their dreams, revealing secrets, promising revenge.

Months later, on the opening day of the redesigned avenue, a neighbour jumped off the roof of the building, and her body—she'd wrapped herself in a white sheet, refusing to witness the fall—landed a few metres from the

Mayor. By the time autumn came, everyone had forgotten about Carmen, about Alicia and Eva, about the man who hanged himself on the hill, and by then, they had already moved on to another life.

TEMPERANCE

Madrid, 1975

L EGS UP, María orders, a fine layer of baby powder coating the skin of her hands. Please. Legs up, it's easier for me that way. Good. That's right. She cleaned her during her bath, and now she just needs her to lie down so she can put the nappy on; otherwise, she'd have put out a towel so the quilt wouldn't get dirty. She warmed up a little water—sometimes she gets it from the tap in the bathtub, or else she heats it on the stove, as when making the tea—dipped a rag in and passed it over her bottom, lathered a little soap on, wiped that away with another wet rag. The nappy—a scrap of coarse fabric, maybe part of an old bed sheet, little use for absorbing shit or piss—she fastens with practised ease, that of somebody who goes through these motions several times a day, day after day, and indeed has been doing so—with the same person—for years. The body horizontal on the bed, eyes closed—those eyes never meet María's, it's as if she wants to erase her from the scene: a strange logic, this, it seems to María, the idea that if we can't see something, it doesn't exist. Legs up, María says. Legs up, and she raises her bottom and arches her back, which is hard work for her and sometimes draws a moan, and then María quickly slides the cloth between her body and the bed, legs down, and slips the rest of the fabric between her thighs, knotting it at one hip, then the other. María offers her hands, beckoning for her to sit up: she reaches out, clamps her fists around the sides of María's hands, squeezes with her thumbs, and María pulls her forward. They come into equilibrium. María turns away, stops looking at the old woman's body—barely able to hold itself upright at the edge of the bed, hands barely able to grip the quilt— ignoring the fact the fabric wouldn't save her fall, that if she lost her balance, the blanket would go with her, maybe the sheet, too. For a moment, turning to look for the woman's clothes, María imagines the body landing on the floor: flesh and old bones, barely flesh enough, skin dry and cracked. If the woman's body were to fall while María—back turned—were looking for underwear, knee-high socks, a dress to wear today, would she realize? Would she mistake it for some other object, something hitting the floor in a neighbouring apartment? Something in the apartment above, a book falling from someone's lap: would Doña Sisi's weight, a few centimetres from where she is, sound the same as the weight of an object several metres overhead? Air and distance, the body of Doña Sisi—a high-pitched whine, maybe a cry to get María's attention: Girl, María, I've hurt myself. Under the sheet, under the bedspread, naked—a rough cloth nappy, an infant eighty years old—on the cold wooden floorboards.

Bathing her each day, María looks at her body: she evaluates damage, compares today's body with yesterday's. She notices when there's a new injury, or when the one from days before has scabbed over, and some weeks, she thinks of telling the woman's daughter about her rapid decline. She helps her in—carefully—and grants the woman some time alone, five or ten minutes while the water cools. Early on, María would ask if she wanted to listen to music, and she would leave her the little transistor radio from the kitchen; later, she noticed the woman didn't much care if she sat in silence or with the radio on, and she saved herself the trip. Then, when she guesses the water is turning lukewarm, María kneels next to the tub and scrubs her with the wash mitt, scrubbing skin that is shrivelled and yet at the same time stretched tight across the bones, and completely hairless. The skin also shows finest threads of dried blood, so faint they never even quite scab up: it's as if they're opening over and over, again and again, maybe the same blood but different. María's movements are more gentle than efficient: she slides the wash mitt over her skin, arm down, torso up, tries to get the woman to be still, she hasn't yet gotten used to the breasts or the pubic area, nor has she gotten used to the shame—she thinks she never will. Her hair, they decided to cut it a few months ago, she'd been pulling out little white fistfuls during arguments; since then, every fifteen or twenty days, when it grew out and began to cover her ears and the nape of her neck, María would carefully trim it. María avoids her eyes as she rinses out the shampoo then pats her dry little by little: her face—her skin is dry here, too, and wrinkled, skin against skin around her eyes and mouth—then the rest of her body. All right, here we go, María always tells her, or we're done now, or any other phrase that will signal to the woman—will remind her, for the moment—that it's her turn to do something, to reach out and wrap her arms around María's neck: she gropes at the emptiness until she can feel the girl, and then María, as best she can, grabs hold of her body, wraps a towel around her, carries her from the bathroom to the bedroom. She tries not to move her as she would an inanimate bundle, but instead to bring a certain delicacy to the task, sometimes she fakes a laugh, or she hums, to lighten things; she manoeuvres her so that she doesn't slip from her grasp and doesn't drip anywhere either, which would mean María having to retrace her steps to wipe up what would otherwise dry and leave a mark. From the moment they undress her for the bath until the clean nappy is on and María has dressed her, the woman keeps her eyes closed: if she's able to avoid seeing her naked body, if she's unaware of the person bathing her naked body, the scene never happened.

As the old woman gets older, the weight slips off her, the memory falters: when María first started coming to their apartment, the mother was still showering alone, still having friends over some afternoons. Their conversations carried all the way to the kitchen; the things they said, and the way they said them, put María inside some of the movies they showed in theatres a few streets over. They reviewed the calendar of saints' days, complained about their ailments, delighted in anecdotes from decades past: parties, dresses, jewellery, oh the mediocrity of the present day compared with the fifties, oh the pure joy of all that had happened in their lives. It wasn't curiosity their chatter provoked in María, but an unfamiliar rage, different from the other kinds of anger she'd experienced. María thought about what that era had been like for her: she knew no more about the thatched one-room

house of her earliest years than what her mother had told her,
back when they still talked, but she retained a memory of the
quagmire the new neighbourhood became after heavy rain,
and of chilly Sundays spent strolling the tree-lined avenue,
families having extended lunches, or summer mornings at
the mill; one day they forbade swimming there, before Chico
was even old enough to go.

The daughter recited the rosary every morning; the
mother joined in for the litany and avoided the mysteries,
the other prayers. During that time, María was not to have
the radio on; she blocked out the voices and set about scrubbing pots and pans, or she went down to do the shopping.
Mother and daughter also parted ways in the afternoon:
until they tore down the church next to Argüelles, the mother
and her friends would go up Calle Princesa arm in arm,
stopping in one or another of the nearby tea rooms; the
Señora's daughter crossed over to San Marcos or went down
as far as the church of Santa Teresa y San José. First one
of the old women died; a few months later, another; then
there were more absences: some got sick and could only
manage the walk from their bedrooms to their bathrooms,
and others began to notice Sisi's first lapses: an incorrect
word, difficulty pronouncing a certain name. The mother
was left alone with her daughter. If María hadn't been dusting the silver frames, she would have been convinced that
the two of them were the outcome of some experiment.
But the photos showed an insubstantial man, with the thin-
nest moustache, no matter the era: thin with the Señora's
arm in his on their wedding day; gossamer in the boats at
the Retiro, Doña Sisi with a head of curls and a little girl

in her arms; virtually see-through in the most recent one, where the daughter from before is already a model of the daughter today, and her mother still has a certain elegance, the brooch, the exaggerated smile. There was a father, those three photos prove it. What happened to him, how he disappeared, María never found out.

The daughter was terrified that the church her mother went to would come crashing down on her head; it had been restored after the war, but she still refused to go along, preferring to walk in the other direction, though avoiding an untimely death under the rubble meant abandoning her mother. She also made sure no men came into the apartment when she was there—since by then the mother was sick, María dealt with the plumber and saw him paid—and had María go back to the drawing board any time she cooked meat on the days in the Catholic calendar when it was forbidden. But there was one thing about the daughter's suspicions and hang-ups that put María at ease: under no circumstances was María to stay overnight. That was made clear from the moment the woman's neighbour—whom one of her aunt's friends had worked for—recommended her, for fear that María might rob them while they slept, or use a pillow to take revenge for whatever trauma she'd dragged along from previous generations, or whatever else that girl from—where was it again?—might be capable of. The daughter never let María vary her routine: she'd walk from the Ópera metro stop, change out of her street clothes and into her uniform, clean and mop and iron and cook, confirm once during each visit that Doña Sisi could still remember certain last names and numbers, later make sure she didn't try to heat up her coffee herself, and finally, bathe and dress her, change her out of that coarse fabric. Surely there were disposable nappies, soft like the ones for babies, but bigger—I can ask, María offered. The daughter said no, condemning her mother to skin irritation all night long, and the smell of shit and urine that often seeped through the sheets to the mattress. Although María had forbidden herself from becoming attached to the families she served—she'd already failed once in this, with the little boy at the first house; keep your distance, the other girls warned when they crossed paths at the market, you're going out the same way you came in—every morning she felt something for Doña Sisi, whose lucidity failed her at times, but who, at others, closed her eyes because, as we know, what we can't see doesn't exist. Not pity, not shame; neither pity nor shame, exactly.

"Today is my saint's day," the mother announced.

María hadn't realized: she'd never heard the name before that first day at the apartment on Calle Ventura de Rodríguez, the day they met her, told her how much they would pay, the dos and don'ts. Not counting the rosaries, the daughter spoke more words at that first meeting than she ever did again. She generally spoke in very short sentences, only telling her what to do and how. María told her that she was living with her aunt and uncle in Carabanchel, that she wasn't from Madrid. She didn't mention Carmen, whom she always omitted, or Pedro, whom she was yet to meet at that point. Do you believe in the mercy of God? the daughter wanted to know; of course, María answered. Years later, when the mother got sick, María came to understand the full extent of her own response. Not exactly pity, not exactly shame:

mercy. Mercy not for all the women giving orders and paying salaries, of course, but for the mother herself.

"My saint is today."

María asked her to pick out a dress for herself, along with a pendant or ring from her jewellery box; she asked if she wanted help putting on some eye make-up or lipstick, but Doña Sisi never responded. To begin with, when the daughter would go to mass early for confession and before the Señora's friends arrived, María and she would chat. They preferred the sound of their voices to the radio: they talked about the weather, what one would cook and the other would eat the next day, Doña Sisi insisted María tell her about her childhood, which she considered exotic, so many people in a house that small, and you're telling me you would sew, with those unsightly hands and those short little fingers of yours? Doña Sisi, where did your nickname come from? The movie? It's Sisi, she corrected, a single *s* and a single *s*; whereas it's the Empress *Sissi*. From Sisinia, after Sisinio. He was the Pope for twenty days, back at the start of the eighth century. He was stricken with gout and had to rely on others to feed him. My father found it funny. Every 23rd November, the mother and daughter went out to dinner to celebrate; when the mother got sick and it was no longer wise for her to set foot outside the apartment, the daughter insisted on a meal that would make up for her confinement. María went to great lengths: she roasted a quarter chicken for the daughter, and another so the mother could have a consommé, made pureed vegetables for the mother and glazed vegetables for the daughter, she prepared a dessert—custard the first year, the daughter didn't like it and demanded María do something more elegant—that Doña Sisi could safely eat.

"When will my daughter be back?"

María lied: soon, she said, though she didn't know. She chose a long-sleeved dress for the woman, burgundy, the fabric thick to keep the chill off her; she put on her slip, her stockings, her dress, and her shoes, and the woman held out her hands so María could help her along, and together, they walked to the living room. She took María's arm and, with tiny steps, they crossed that apartment, high-ceilinged and dimly lit—no cleaning product could ever brighten those windows—with its three-bedroom wing down the hall. The door to the master bedroom, where the father used to sleep, they kept closed; María went in some mornings to dust and air it out. On either side were the wife's room and the daughter's, with identical furniture; the mother's always with a vase of flowers that María tried to keep fresh, though Doña Sisi no longer noticed either way. One foot then the other, step by step to the living room, until the Señora collapses onto the sofa; she covers her with a blanket to keep her warm, because María wouldn't want to deal with the old woman catching cold, too. María turns on the television and goes to the kitchen, a chamomile tea for Doña Sisi—she'll keep an eye on her while she drinks it—a coffee for herself. Sometimes, while the daughter is on her way back, she and the Señora sit in front of the TV and watch whatever's on; when she hears the lift approaching the third floor, María gets up and goes back to the kitchen, just in case. What struck

María about the teas she hosted in those first years was how Doña Sisi embellished every story: there were other, bigger apartments in the building, of course, furnished more luxuriously—María could tell when she went down for milk or salt, doing the best she could with the money they gave her for the shopping—but the mother outdid them all with her descriptions; she convinced them of a glorious past.

"Turn off the TV. There's something happening in the street."

They received María that Thursday with the curtains drawn, no TV and no music, at most, a radio talk show; don't speak unless it's absolutely necessary, in this household, we respect the dead: the daughter bid complete silence and left the house at midmorning. When lunchtime came and went, spoonful after spoonful of soup for the mother, María taking hers in the kitchen, she understood the daughter wouldn't be eating at home and put some aside for her, in case she came back later wanting some food. The daughter showed up a few minutes before the appointed end of María's shift—María concerned she'd have to stay late so that Doña Sisi wouldn't be alone. The daughter asked, Are you going through Ópera? María thought at first that she was warning her to avoid it because of all the people, but then she understood that the question had an ulterior meaning: are you going to the lying-in-state, the daughter wanted to know. María said yes; yes, of course: she understood that was what was expected. The daughter said she was pleased to hear it, pleased to know she was a decent woman, and when María left the building, she did initially go in the direction of Ópera, down Calle de Ferraz, but changed her mind when she got to Plaza de España and went up to Gran Vía instead, followed it to Callao, and got on the metro home. María counted on those Saturday and Sunday afternoons, all she had to do was make a little food that the daughter could heat up on her own, but the daughter had warned her before she left: such strange times we're living in, I'm sure you can imagine; we may need you around to take care of the Señora a little more. The Señora, her mother. María had no idea what her reasons were, but she said yes, of course. On Sunday, when she came in through the service door in the kitchen, as she did every day, it wasn't the daughter's prayers that that she heard, but the mother's wailing, with a nappy that could have been full for any amount of time.

"Where did you come from?"

Some mornings the woman would ask her that: where did you come from, how did you get here. María doesn't know if she's returning to the formality of the first few years, but instead of asking about the weather, getting confused and thinking of geography instead; if she's mistaking her for the daughter; or if she simply sees her face anew each day. María describes her route patiently: the building entrance, the streets, the metro stop, the recurring faces in the metro carriage. Met with indifference from Doña Sisi—María can't tell if she isn't listening, isn't interested, or if she forgets one day to the next—she makes revisions to her story: she doesn't wake up in her apartment, but in her aunt and uncle's, where she was still living when she took the job, or she tells her everything she remembers about the stretch between her parents' house and the workshop. The endless street with its cheap limewashed facades, some identical, impossible to tell apart without looking at the number—and some owners were reluctant to hang up the glazed tiles—or listening to the conversations taking place inside. The endless street that led to another one just the same, the memory isn't tinged with the grey of the concrete in Madrid—the colour she thinks of when she thinks of roadways or pavement—but with the umber of the soil in her neighbourhood. It's not your neighbourhood any more, she tells herself when, in her story for Doña Sisi, she closes the door, hurries along until the houses run out and turns left, towards the bus stop. As the bus drives on, the houses stop looking like the house where Soledad and Chico and their parents live—in the memory, Carmen hasn't been born yet—and she has the feeling that those images belong to another place, that the window isn't transparent and that the buildings and people she sees are projected onto it instead, like in a cinema. She didn't belong to the city of the houses she sees from inside the bus, of those buildings near the workshop, and what she guessed was happening inside; nor did she belong to the city of the first house where she worked, the one with the sweet-smelling boy, nor to Doña Sisi and her daughter's dark apartment. She'll figure that out afterwards, of course, she'll think about all that later; right now, María talks, and Doña Sisi looks at the empty TV screen, the empty vase, and sometimes she says "that's nice," or "well, you're here now," "would you like a glass of water," or sometimes she says nothing at all.

Thursday night Pedro came over to tell her, in case she hadn't heard. The whole country knows, she snapped—as she did in other moments when she felt him talking down to her. And so since Friday, María has stopped getting off at Ópera and walking along the edge of the square, but transfers at Callao instead, to the yellow line that drops her on the corner of the street, or goes up Gran Vía, looking in the shop windows. Pedro had warned her not to go near the Plaza de Oriente, and María promised to avoid it but said that she would have to work out some way of getting to the apartment. Since the daughter didn't turn up on Friday, didn't turn up on Saturday, and hasn't turned up today, either, María decides she won't keep to the kitchen, and serves herself at the table in the living room instead. The daughter had spent all of Friday waiting to get into the lying-in-state, and on Saturday went back again, and took part in the prayers being held at the parish church, as well. Would she be going to a church closer to home again today, or would she have convinced some neighbours to make room for her in their car so she could go all the way up to Cuelgamuros? María hasn't asked, the daughter hasn't said: her handbag, her coat, the door slamming shut. Neither mother nor daughter says a word: on the shelves, photographs almost without context, some of the man María guesses is husband and father. She's never dared to ask if he's still alive, and none of the girls from the other apartments know a thing. They usually only last a few years: working in domestic service and getting married and then it's domestic service in their own homes, or tiring of it, taking domestic service work elsewhere, all of them very young, from Cádiz, Murcia, Badajoz. Instead of referring to one another by name, they use the names of the apartments where they clean and mop and cook, María bathes and changes the Señora; the one from the first-floor apartment on the right can't stand the twins; in the apartment upstairs, nobody lasts more than a few months. When María stops working there, none of them will ever hear anything about her again: she'll disappear, as if she had never existed.

María hears the sound of the lift, and judging by the time that's passed, thinks it could be the daughter; but rather than stopping at their floor it keeps on going to the one above, and María can relax. She retraces her steps—she'd been on her way back to the kitchen already—and looks in on the Señora lying on the sofa, blanket draped haphazardly over her body. Although she hasn't asked her anything, and María doesn't make a habit of speaking unless spoken to—a few reassuring words, sometimes, when she's bathing or changing or dressing her, to soothe her—something about the silence now is discomfiting. There's not much to do: Doña Sisi is dressed, the house is clean, and there's time yet before she needs to start making lunch and whatever she's going to leave for dinner. The Señora asked her to turn off the TV so she could hear what was happening in the street, not realizing that the images on the screen and the sounds were connected, and when María turned it back on again, the old woman said no: narrowing her eyes and, with some effort, waving her right hand from side to side. Although the Señora has shown no interest in what's happening, María doesn't know what else to talk about and settles on describing the things they've seen on TV: she admits that she's been impressed by the queues of people, one small body after another, from the palace on, snaking far into the distance beyond Santa

Teresa y San José; small bodies that could for all the world belong to Doña Sisi and her daughter, and herself, as well, Pedro, her parents.

The daughter still isn't back, and María has nothing else to say. With lunchtime still a distant prospect, she disobeys the old woman and switches the TV back on, background noise. She looks at Doña Sisi, her eyes closed, dozing on the couch: not so unusual, she has slept a great deal since she got sick, because of the medication or because of her age or because there's not much to do besides closing her eyes to keep from seeing, sleep, open her eyes, sleep again. María sits back down next to her on the sofa; instinctively reaches out for her hand—for the first time, no idea why—she searches under the blanket and feels that her hand is cold. Not so surprising, given the temperature outside, the logic of the weather: the end of November, Sunday 23rd, Saint Sisinia's day. The Señora is still sleeping, or so it appears: she taps her shoulder gently, the fingertips of her right hand—her left poised over the cold hand—touching her shoulder, hesitant at first, then insistent; the woman is unresponsive. María says her name, Doña Sisi, a whisper in case she's asleep, and then again, Sisi, Sisi, she repeats, the name becomes a conjunction that signals a desire: María doesn't want what she thinks has happened to happen. Her voice loud, louder each time: Doña Sisi, Sisi, Señora, say something, the slumped body lolling away from her, flesh and old bones, barely flesh enough, skin dry and cracked. María lets go of the old woman's hand, moves back, thinks about what to do. What to do, María: get help, find someone. A phone call? Who could she call? Chico? Pedro? Her uncle, who she's hardly seen since she left that first apartment for her own? Get help, find someone: the caretaker, some neighbour. A man would know what to do.

She doesn't use the service exit because some of the girls have Sundays off, and it's possible no one would hear her. She leaves the door open, leaves the unresponsive Doña Sisi on the sofa, her body slumped over to the left, bones and flesh and taut skin that María refuses to think of as coming apart, devoured by worms; she puts the house keys in the pocket of her apron and doesn't wait for the lift, taking the stairs down to the caretaker's office at a run instead. The office is closed: Sunday, nobody home. María knocks on the caretaker's door, the dull thud of her closed fist against the door, rap, rap rap, rap rap rap, louder and louder each time, open up, listen, it's María, Doña Sisi's María, from the third floor, her voice louder and louder, you have to help me: no one answers. Her ear against the door: nothing. María takes one step back, then another, runs upstairs to the first floor, rings the doorbell on the left and then the one on the right, her breathing ragged from the effort and the fear, open up, she repeats, listen, it's María, Doña Sisi's María, help, it's an emergency. It's the same story as downstairs: no one answers, the caretaker doubtless off enjoying a family Sunday, safely ensconced in the home of some relative in another neighbourhood, wife and children in front of plates of rice in Villaverde Bajo, what a nice Sunday for the families in 1A and 1B, she has no difficulty imagining them on the crowded pavement alongside Doña Sisi's daughter, waving white handkerchiefs in the air, tears running from the corners of their eyes to their chins. María, meanwhile, tears through the building: the first-floor apartments empty, she goes up to the second floor. Breathless, she knocks on 2A, repeats her message, listen, open up, Doña Sisi, emergency, hey, hey: no answer on that side of the landing. María holds the buzzer down, turns and crosses to 2B, banging on the door, yelling help, yelling emergency, it's María, Doña Sisi's María, open up. She doesn't notice that she's using the possessive, that she understands herself as belonging to the Señora; she doesn't think about that, not in that moment, not during those years. Finally, she hears something: a noise, a shifting chair or table, wood against wood, flesh and bones other than Doña Sisi's bones against the upholstery. Coming, the voice on the other side announces as the door—one lock, and another, and a chain—opens.

"I'm María, Doña Sisi's girl, from the third floor. The Señora isn't answering me. Something's happened to her, she's not talking to me, I shake her, and nothing happens. Help me, please."

"The family isn't home. They went up to El Escorial… I don't know if I can leave the apartment. They'll be back soon."

María says please. She says please, nothing more; she knows that the way she's looking at the woman adds something, that her difficulty breathing—she's nearly heaving—adds something, her body, hanging from the door frame, adds something. The woman who works in 2B says yes, says OK, and guesses that if the family comes back, they'll hear the commotion upstairs and go and investigate. She closes the door—this takes time: one lock, then another—and follows María up the stairs, María taking them two at a time, the woman from the second floor, one, then another. The floor plans are different—the woman had heard that the apartments on the left side of the building were a little more modest, one balcony fewer—and she runs her eye over the furniture, quickly appraising the care the Señora has taken looking after it all. On the sofa?, the woman asks. María has heard that she sleeps in a cubbyhole off the kitchen, and is a little older than her: no one would call her the 2B *girl*. Yes, María says, on the sofa. The woman picks her way between the furniture and approaches Doña Sisi, the blanket covering up the cold of the floor. She leans over her, and María guesses that the woman's hand must be feeling for her wrist, her neck. María hadn't been mistaken when she'd checked before, touching her shoulder, her cold hand; in a way, she'd needed someone else to confirm it. She's having trouble breathing; she has taken the apron off and thrown it to the floor, as if the strap around her neck had been tightening, but it's still hard for her to breathe.

"María," the woman comes towards her. "I'm so sorry, María. There's no pulse. She's not breathing. I'm so sorry, I really am."

The conversations that filled the emptiness of Doña Sisi's final lucid days come back to María in a jumble, including Doña Sisi telling María the story behind her name. She knew already that it had been chosen by her father—her father, two words that always stood alone: the Señora never went into detail about him, never divulged his name or background or profession, and there wasn't a single photograph anywhere in the apartment of anyone besides the mother, the daughter, and the absent husband. He came up with it by adapting the name of a male saint who'd had a brief, sickly spell as Pope. But I only know of one mention of the saint, Saint Sisinia—and at this point she lowered her voice—and it comes from a prayer to exorcize the devil. She glanced from side to side, checking her daughter hadn't returned from mass unnoticed—sometimes she shut herself up in her room when she got back, didn't come out even for lunch or dinner—and she explained to María that there are only two women capable of facing the possessed: Our Lady, and Saint Sisinia. Jesus and the Baptist, the archangels and martyrs, the prophets and the hierarchs, all of them—all men—are mentioned, but you only invoke them. Our Lady, Christ's mother, is asked to do something else, to summon the power of the Word and the Cross, but it's Saint Sisinia who actually casts the devil out. She can do what no man, no other saint, is able to: force the devil out of the bodies of the possessed. To my father, that was funny. What about you, María? Where did your name come from? My grandmother's name was María, she was also my godmother. How nice, María, the old woman said, smiling; if the devil knocks on our door one day, between the two of us, we'll send him packing. While the downstairs maid asks what to do, what can I do, call the hospital, the funeral home, nothing like this has ever happened to me, and on today of all days; honey, this isn't my dead; María doesn't understand her use of the possessive, it's as if Doña Sisi's corpse belonged to María. By the time the recollection has run its course, the woman has already gone for the phone, and María listens to her speaking. She calls a doctor for the dead body, as if the saints in that gloomy apartment could spark a miracle.

"Yes, I'm calling from 3, Ventura Rodríguez, apartment 3B. The Señora isn't breathing, she's unresponsive, she doesn't have a pulse. Yes, I know you can't get here. But didn't Oriente empty out a while ago?"

If you ask me, there must be other people dying in Madrid today, either that or they've forbidden people from dying until he's done being buried; the woman—who tries not to say "Franco," to avoid problems—thereby forcing complicity on María, who looks at her unseeingly: eyes straight ahead now, first on the woman standing in front of the coffee table, then on Doña Sisi on the sofa. María doesn't respond, and they haven't closed the door to the apartment, and the woman says she's sorry if anyone's heard them from the landing, or if they lose their trust in María, or if the old woman regains consciousness—it's eerie how hard it is to tell a living person from a dead one: she cooks and cleans, what does she know of such things—and denounces her to her family. There, the possessive again; again, one the property of another. María says nothing, and the woman tries again, my God, María, I'm so sorry, what are you going to do, the woman tries to comfort her while María observes *her dead* from a distance. Is this death *hers*, then? How are she and Doña Sisi connected? The light filtering in from the street doesn't even indicate midday, but to María and the woman from 2B, it feels much later. It's not the light, not even the windows: María blames it—almost night-time in here—on the colour of the furniture, their uniforms, the dress she chose for Doña Sisi. She blames it on the dead body crumpled against the left arm of the sofa, flesh and old bones, shrivelled skin stretched tight across bones, barely a dent in the old sofa from the non-existent weight of her, María thinks of the old woman's tendency to close her eyes to what was going on around her: if I don't see it, it doesn't exist. Someone comes into the apartment—a doctor or the daughter, the caretaker, the family from the apartment downstairs come to demand their meal from their girl—she doesn't notice: María opens her eyes wide.

THE HANGED MAN

Córdoba, 1999

N OW HER BODY'S HANGING from a beam in the assembly hall: someone tied her hands behind her back,
they've hung her by the right ankle, tightly enough that the
knot won't slip and let her body go crashing to the ground.
Because that, of course, would mean physical injury, the pain
of the impact, maybe a broken bone—the distance between
the ceiling and floor is not great, making more serious consequences unlikely—and whoever tied up the teenager only
wants to embarrass her. No one knows how long the girl has
been there: no classes have been held there all day, and her
English teacher swears he crossed paths with her on his way
in, but they do know that she's been absent from three classes
in a row. Since she gets the highest marks in her exams and
turns in her homework on time—well written and, though
she misses a comma here and there, showing a willingness
and an ability to reflect—no one is alarmed. A cold, a routine
medical appointment, she'll be back tomorrow to explain,
no chance she's loitering in some square smoking cigarettes,
or down at the shopping centre. Even the brightest student
sometimes feels like disappearing for a day, they understand

and turn a blind eye; but in fact she's been hidden away in this place, upside down, hanging by one ankle.

A teacher from the language and literature department, not one of her teachers, discovers her, there to set up in advance of a big lecture that day: the floral arrangement she'd planned to present to the lecturer drops from her hands, flowers and dirt and lumps of clay scattering across the tiles. Are the girl's eyes open? Are her lips moving? She can't see: she's been strung up with her back to the door. The teacher asks if she's alive, Alicia says yes. She doesn't ask if she's OK—she isn't—but if she's breathing, if she's conscious. The teacher goes to her, relieved—she hasn't stumbled upon the corpse of a student—and turns the girl towards her: the skin of her face red, the pupils fixed on hers. I'm Alicia, from 3B. Her voice trembles because of the position she's in, from the time spent upside down, but she maintains a neutral tone: having calmly introduced herself, she looks at the teacher and waits for her reaction. The woman goes away and comes back—Alicia works out that maybe ten minutes pass, one, one thousand; two, one thousand; three, one thousand; four, one thousand; she counts the seconds and gets bored around five hundred—accompanied by several other teachers, the caretaker, and three students in their final year, hauling in a mat from the gym. The caretaker takes a minute or two to bring a ladder, and by the time one of the teachers gets the knot around her ankle untied, Alicia sees the head teacher crossing himself: from a distance, as if he's watching them act out a scene. Will he applaud at the end? The teacher who found her notes that she was hung skilfully—whoever did it took care to ensure that the knot could sustain sixty kilos of teenager and hardly leave a mark. She says as much under her breath, trusting that no one will hear, but everyone else's silence amplifies the sound. A few of the teachers—she recognizes the one who teaches French—hold her under the shoulders so she doesn't crash to the floor; the students have placed the mat under her, to cushion the fall should they fail to catch her. While they take her down, Alicia thinks she deserved it. Once she's been untied, they all hold her in place as she regains her balance; they lay her down on the mat, and Alicia looks at them from her position on the floor, one face and another and another, one alongside the next, most of them still without the faintest idea of what has gone on.

The teacher is still up on the ladder. She asks Alicia if she wants to keep the rope, as a memento.

She's right to think she deserved it: she's been provoking her classmates since day one, humiliating them, mocking them, and even worse, she's enjoyed it. Always her way. In primary school they'd respond with violence, waiting at the classroom door with fists aimed at her stomach, someone spewing insults, fucking bitch, someone else grabbing her ponytail, pulling the scrunchie clean off, along with a few tangled hairs; she'd been hoping for a more sophisticated response from these classmates, and as it turned out they had been up to the task. She wasn't mistaken, even if deep down it's hard for her to accept. The first one got the pleasure of seeing her suffer a little—right at the start, when they'd just hung her up and her head was still pounding—but the rest of the plan, she applauds: seamless. It doesn't matter if your father sells staplers in a neighbourhood with no bus stops or if there's a law firm with his name on it. They say money doesn't transform mediocrity, but Alicia knows that's not true. At the very least, money tempers it, helps to conceal it: it gets you a weekly allowance, which you can use to buy rope; a private internet connection—not the public one at the library, where whoever logs on next can see your search history—so you can research the most secure knots.

The head teacher begs her not to say anything in class, so the parents won't find out what happened. A teacher she recognizes—she once stood in for the social studies teacher— holds out a hand to help her up. Alicia feels dizzy and grabs her arm to avoid falling: the students lead her over to a chair, and one of them decides to say something. You were asking for it. Alicia looks around, none of the teachers are there to hear; all of them, except the language and literature one— who is already setting chairs out in front of the stage—are gone. Alicia looks at the guy, who she's never seen before, and says yes. Yes, she says proudly: I deserved it, like someone accepting a prize. Come on, a round of applause.

In the following days, Alicia sticks to her version: she doesn't remember anything, she opened her eyes and sud- denly found herself in the assembly hall, upside down and hanging by the ankle, the ceiling on the floor and the floor on the ceiling, and on the horizon, the empty stage. Who did it, Alicia? I don't remember. How did they do it? I don't remember. When? I don't remember. The facts the priests mull over—years later, Alicia will cast her mind back to the head teacher crossing himself as they lowered her to the ground—have been supplied by others: the teacher who said hello to her that day as she entered the building and who swears it must all have happened no earlier than a quarter past eight; a couple of classmates, also solitary types, who insist she didn't even make it to her desk, because they would have noticed, but say that's all they know. There was a moment before the bell rang for first period, there was a space between the entrance gate and the assembly hall —at the far end of the building, past the library and the staff room and the offices—and whoever hung the girl up had slipped through those gaps. Was it a joke? Something she herself arranged with an accomplice as a way of getting attention, had it got out of hand, was she now trying to protect them so they wouldn't give her away? If they knew Alicia, if they'd gone to the trouble of listening to her, they would have realized that she found almost nothing funny. Her classmates don't reveal anything either. No one snitches on anyone, no one confesses, and no one asks what happened to Alicia, who, for her part, never goes back to class.

Alicia had gone into the year almost certain of it: everyone would know her story. It had been in the papers: the businessman who, faced with financial ruin, tried to make his suicide look like an accident. Surely her classmates' parents would have mentioned it at home: that poor girl, look where they're living now. At that point, they weren't guaranteed a place at any of the state schools, so their mother had kept them enrolled at the Carmelite school: and from then on—in her past life, it had been afternoons and nights, but in her future life, after her father's death, once they were in the neighbourhood on the outskirts and their mother was working in Uncle Chico's kitchen, it was mornings—Alicia would go out of her way to pass by the apartment. To show her sister the place they'd never moved to, to make sure she didn't forget. Eva would whine, pull on her trouser leg or her sleeve, and in the end just break off from her sister and walk the rest of the way to school alone. Alicia stayed to scrutinize the balcony, the windows, what was happening inside. Who was there in their place?

But Alicia's suspicion was unwarranted: she'd spent several terms with the same classmates; it was their indifference, not her circumstances or backstory, that made it so hard for her to feel like part of the group. To them, Alicia was inconsequential, she didn't exist, no one cared: just one girl approached her, on the second day, and told her in a whisper that her father had known Alicia's. Alicia found out that this girl's father was a bank manager, and that was enough for her to never speak to the girl, Marina, again, and start working out ways she could hurt simple, naive Marina, Marina the animal lover; how Alicia relished the day when a rat slipped into the classroom through a crack in the wall, coming and going as it pleased for an entire period, lingering near the girl, her tears when the teacher found out. No one so much as spoke to Alicia, and she made no overtures herself: she would talk her way out of required group projects, since she lived in another neighbourhood; she used its distance from the school, like her responsibilities, as an excuse: I take care of my sister, I can't leave her alone and come back here. The teachers didn't stand in her way. Her classmates would walk home in their groups, and the two of them still had a journey of thirty or forty minutes ahead. Eva took too long saying goodbye to her friends, a kiss on each cheek and a hug and a promise that she would call later, and Alicia waited patiently so they could walk down to the bus stop.

During this time, Alicia dreamt of her father every night: her father's suicide, hanging himself from a tree after the botched car crash, every single night until her alarm clock went off in the morning, and Alicia ran her fingers across her neck and stretched her legs to make sure she was alive. She never said a word to anyone. Who could she have told? She was surrounded by friends she didn't have, a mother who never spoke, an uncle who worked all hours, her little sister. Alicia woke up to the alarm or the noise of her mother's high heels, to the sound of the bracelets on her mother's wrists, any noise in any room in the tiny apartment: the bedroom or the bathroom, the kitchen. Their mother got ready to go to the bar and told them to get dressed and eat breakfast, blew them kisses and closed the door with relief: they wouldn't see one another again until lunchtime, when they would come to the bar for the daily special, and after that, not until late in the evening; with any luck, they'd be asleep by the time she got back smelling of rancid oil. Alicia would make sure of it: when it was almost ten o' clock, she brushed her teeth, changed out of her tracksuit and into pyjamas, and said goodnight to Eva, who was absorbed in whatever was on TV, nodding off on the sofa almost every night so she could hug her mother before she went to bed, Eva kissing strangers, Eva pulling everyone close, whether or not they merited it. Even if she couldn't sleep, during those months, Alicia would lie in bed with the light turned off, waiting in silence for the bad dream to come: eyes closed, the image of the dry earth in the days leading up to summer, her father's suicide recreated scene by scene.

What does everyone else dream about? On the bus to school, Alicia hears people say that their teeth fall out, that they're walking down the street naked, that they miss trains or have to retake exams they've already passed. At home, she looks up symbols in a dream dictionary she bought at a second-hand book fair: fear of change, concern about a challenging time, ups and downs in a relationship. Men and women, children and adults: no one confesses to dreaming of anything else. She has memorized other people's dreams—the simple descriptions; the details they emphasize, thinking them unique—in case she needs to include them in conversations she never actually has, applying the different interpretations to her own circumstances. The teeth, the nakedness, arriving late at the station, the pass mark forever just out of reach: that way, her story will seem more plausible. Who would believe her if she told them what really happens?

Her, strung up in the high-school assembly hall: even today, Alicia leaves that out when, over coffee, she goes back to anecdotes from those years, the kind of exchange where you're dusting off a scene before whoever you're talking to has even finished telling you hers. It's not that she's ashamed or embarrassed, it's that she understands the decision—to tell the story, to describe herself going inside the building and how it all started from there, the hours she spent with that rope cutting into the skin of her ankle—will grant the other children a place in her memory. Were they even worth that?

They wanted to feel important, of course: she recognizes the irony, the effort expended in planning; she recognizes that at some point, she underestimated them. She barely recalls more than one or two classmates' names, of course she's forgotten their circumstances, but she does remember how she hurt them, her reasons for spending weeks devising ways to shame them or show them up. Marina, we've already mentioned, that's one name she remembers. There was another girl, with curly hair, who she could tell was laughing at her jeans, worn out and torn at the thighs. Then there was the boy who refused to lend her a tissue when she had a cold—Alicia had to wipe her nose on her jumper, ashamed: when the bell rang for break, she hurried to the bathroom to run the fabric under cold water for minutes, soaked when she got back to class—he made things hard for her: not one false move, not a single moment of clumsiness for her to pick out and attack; for days and days, she observed him in class, even followed him after making sure Eva was all right taking the bus to the bar alone, asked her sister to tell their mother she had a stomach ache, that she'd gone home and would heat up some soup there. Then, one day in maths, jackpot: the boy—Daniel was his name—forgets his book and asks to share with the kid next to him; she wasn't worthy of generosity, but he is. Suddenly, one boy looks at the other, for two or three seconds longer than usual. Alicia sits with that look, and for weeks, she follows the clues: the constant forgetfulness—a pen or correction fluid—his attempts to comment on every football match, the enthusiastic responses to questions asked with indifference, the glances the student next to him never returns, and which the boy who refused to lend her a tissue still thinks nobody notices. He's wrong: Alicia watches him from the back row. Her excuse is that she's the last to arrive, and a little shy, but the previous year she learnt that it's a strategic position, that it gives you an advantage over the rest. Seeing without being seen. Studying the other teenagers, fourteen, fifteen years old: putting yourself, with respect to others, in the only position of privilege your circumstances allow.

Faced with a disadvantage, she had two options: attack or defend. Alicia chose the first. So, kid, who knows what your name is—you're lucky, I remembered: Daniel—who knows who your parents are, where you live, what you'll be doing in a decade or two; so, boy who refused to unzip the pocket of your backpack and take out your tissues and hand one to the girl two rows back when she asked you for it—the girl in front of Alicia, and behind you, Daniel, acted as a link: Alicia forgave her because her nose was running, too, and she'd just finished wiping it on the sleeve of her own jumper—so you're into the guy who sits next to you, it's your turn to be taken down a notch, maybe next time you'll behave a little better, maybe you'll be nice. Alicia knows almost as little about the one as she does about the other: but she understands that in the context of a religious school, there are certain problematic attachments. She contemplates her options for revenge, possible wounds to inflict. Revealing his orientation seems excessive and unfair, and anyway, it's not like her; she's subtler than that. She's not trying to destroy Daniel, future engineer, future auditor, someone who, in ten or twenty years, Alicia might serve a coffee or a steak. Just a lesson, a tug on the ear to get his attention, something to make him think again, to ask her forgiveness for having been so cold. One morning, while she's changing her tampon, Alicia decides: when the bell for break rings—since she has no one to talk to, she usually spends break time in the library—she takes her time packing up, waiting until everyone's gone. She opens her classmate's backpack, takes out a book, sticks it inside, and closes it. No one will rat on her: she acts quickly, then goes out of her way to be seen in the cafeteria, in the bathroom, and in front of the announcement board, looking at information on language exchanges; she also made an appointment with the school counsellor, explaining she was going to be changing schools the following year, and she's having a hard time with everything it entails. No one doubts a poor fatherless girl who's asking for help, struggling to adapt to a new reality, admitting that she's afraid of turning into a troubled teen. In the next class, when the teacher tells them which section to turn to today, Daniel discovers an open menstrual pad stuck to the page, its wings covering up the images, the page will tear if he tries to unstick it. He and the boy next to him see it, so does the girl one row back—we know her already, one of the solitary ones, Alicia cares so little about the girl's existence that she doesn't consider wasting any energy on her—and Alicia, who now regrets not having used the pad before, though the sensationalism isn't in line with her usual work. The boy next to Daniel shifts in his seat, Alicia sees him digging his fingernails into his forearms to keep from laughing; it'll be a long time before Daniel can look him in the eye, if he ever can. Alicia won't be there to see it: by then, they will have hung her by the ankle in the high-school assembly hall, and she'll be staying home for the rest of term.

Attack or self-defence, then: each time her classmates exclude her from their plans, she responds with violence. Alicia doesn't sign up for the field trips to the countryside or discounted theatre tickets, of course, because she has nothing in common with them, plus because she's not sure she can afford it—even at a discount, a night at the theatre costs the same as the entire year's worth of clothes her mother bought her—and she guesses it's the latter that sets her apart: that they don't invite her to birthday parties or the movies because, more than anything else, they know she doesn't have money. They know nothing about her, but they know about jeans worn out at the knees, they know who waits for the bus that goes to the other side of the city. What a shame, poor little poor girl, but Alicia wishes they'd do it, wishes they'd include her: she wishes a classmate would come up to her, excited, tell her that on Saturday they're meeting up at six to go out to the youth club, ask if she wants to join; Alicia wants to sneer with all the superiority she can muster and say no, no, I don't think I'll be wasting my time on you. Maybe a hint of laughter as her full stop, then she'll go back to whatever she was doing, putting her notebooks away, zipping up her pencil case. She demands at least the chance to reject them. Since no one is giving it to her, she'll somehow have to show them she exists, body almost stuck to the back wall of the packed classroom, so far from the teacher's desk that once, raising her hand wasn't enough, and she called out to get his attention. A murmuring in the first few rows, someone says that's not how we do it here, you must have picked that up wherever it is you come from. The teacher clicks his tongue and makes an exception for Alicia, I can barely see who's at the back of the room from up here, what is it you want to know. Alicia explains, taking pleasure in the question—too obvious for a smart girl like her not to have figured out on her own; she sees there's one student who doesn't turn to look at her, and she's convinced they must have been the one who made the remark.

Deep down, in some way, she's proud: of what she's managed to awaken in her classmates, the way they've reacted. Had she really behaved that badly? They had it all worked out, the distance and the weight, the timing: they passed the test. If she were to think about what happened, if in ten or twenty years she were to think about what happened, she'd have two options: pretence or truth. Play the fool, like she had when her teachers questioned her: I don't know who did it, I don't know when they did it, I don't know why. But now for the truth: there were four of them. Were they acting alone, a little gang unto themselves, or on behalf of the entire class who had collectively decided on the best way to shut Alicia up for the rest of the year? Mario—first impressions: he's always talking to Marina, the one who cried over the rat, she of the bank manager father—grabbed her by the hair, to Alicia's delight: just the scandal she'd wanted, to put the Carmelites on the same footing as the state-school kids and their cement playground. They came up behind her: in the main hallway, boys and girls crowded together, coats and pens, backpacks enough that retreat wasn't an option. They made it difficult for her. She walks on because she prefers tension to physical pain, which she doesn't tolerate well.

Mario yanks her towards him by the ponytail, she resists, pulling forward with her head, he shoves her in the back. Alicia tries to go towards the staff room, the offices and the assembly hall, trusting that some adult will see the many hands forcing a classmate along. Grabbing her ponytail is a little excessive—it's four against one—but she understands that Mario likes the idea of the pain he's inflicting on her. Just then, Alicia hears: look at her, not even putting up a fight, going there of her own free will. Mario shifts the force of his left hand, the one pulling her hair, to his right, which is pressing hard against her back. So there's a plan, Alicia thinks; she also thinks things are starting to get interesting. Where, she says, and he answers the assembly hall. Of course, the voice—so far, just one—is linked to a face, a name, a body. She doesn't actually care what they have to say, but in class she always listens, in case there's some detail she can use to her own advantage. Susana, always looking out the corner of her eye, with the best marks in PE: you don't do so well with books, do you. Alicia doesn't remember if she's done anything to her—Alicia to Susana, that is—and she's surprised that Susana agreed to get involved, simple sort of girl that she is. Someone—another voice: Sarita, whose spelling mistakes she made fun of when she went up to write on the blackboard, and who went back to her desk dying of embarrassment and never again volunteered— says open, it's open. The teacher had explained on the first day of school that when the wood swells, the door doesn't shut properly, that sometimes it's hard to open, and they've had to cancel a few lectures over it. A fourth voice—hello, Daniel: I expected you—tells them faster, go faster: they run the risk of getting caught if there's class in there during first period. Now Susana is binding her hands with rope; Alicia lets her do it, she's curious. She looks from one face to the next: they all seem the same, the girls with long, dark hair, the boys' hair short, spiked up with gel. She could swap their faces and identities, and no one would ever notice that the teenager who sits down at their table isn't the one who left home that morning. I have the good rope in my backpack, Mario says. Hurry, get up there. Alicia thinks that whoever climbs onto another classmate's shoulders to tie the rope to the beam must be light and agile: Sarita, probably. They're lucky the ceiling isn't higher, lucky the priests were working within their means, that they'd built two floors in a space that could have fitted one, said no to high ceilings. Really? Was her life really ending here, in the school assembly hall, in front of a painting of Saint John of the Cross lit by a ray that is God himself, hanged by Mario and Susana and Sarita and Daniel? Well, worse things have happened, she thinks, while they turn her upside down. This part does baffle her: the rope doesn't go around her neck, but around her right ankle instead.

When Alicia tells them she doesn't remember, it's because she doesn't remember, and when she tells them she doesn't know, it's because she doesn't know. Or rather, it's not that she doesn't remember or doesn't know, it's just not worth her time to explain to them what happened. The head teacher asks her, adjusting his clerical collar, and Alicia holds firm. One priest asks her, and another, and another, ones she has never seen in the halls before, never heard at daily prayer—they're often made to go to mass, some Sundays she and Eva have to make the bus trip twice to take communion—and Alicia insists that she doesn't remember and doesn't know. One of them says it must be the fear; they shouldn't force her to tell on her classmates, because the sheer terror of it—the sheer terror! Alicia thinks to herself at home that night, holding back her laughter—might have blocked her memory. Who knows what horrors they inflicted upon her, he explains to the others, and after her tragic loss, too; how Our Lord tests us so we can show ourselves worthy. Alicia says of course, yes, quite; aware that, without knowing it, they've provided her with the perfect excuse. If I tell you who did it, Father, how could I ever risk going back to class? Hanging from the beam in the assembly hall, dangling upside down, Alicia heard her classmates scurry off, Mario, Susana, Sarita, Daniel—whose idea could it have been, who got the others onboard?—they shouldered their backpacks, made sure they weren't leaving behind a key chain or pencil case that would give them away. Someone—she couldn't see who: they tied her up facing the stage—had gone to the trouble of folding her jacket over her backpack so no one would steal it. The gesture, she thought later, was touching: they wanted to hurt her, but only up to a certain point. They had trouble open-ing the door, which they'd closed so no one would burst in on them. When she heard it slam shut, she closed her eyes, waited patiently for someone to find her and get her down. It was several hours—she swears she slept a little—before a teacher wanted to impress a lecturer she admired and took advantage of her free period to set out chairs, to place flowers at the foot of the stage, to find Alicia hanging from a rope.

————

Some time before, as Mario and Susana and Sarita and Daniel were giving each other instructions, Alicia interrupted:

"My father hanged himself. By the neck. If you guys really want to have a laugh at my expense, you've missed that little detail. Get on with it."

They didn't hear her or pretended not to have heard her. They laughed. They went silent. They said they thought the others would be impressed. Is that what it was about? Do they talk about it now with their friends, years later, over coffee? Do they remember Alicia at all?

THE BATTLE

Madrid, 1982

HERE YOU GO, MARÍA: your beer. Why? What are we drinking to? Who ordered a beer? A beer, today of all days. We should be drinking wine. Or champagne, like the French! That's where they're all coming from, over there! Three beers! Didn't know what I was getting myself into, coming here with you! I'm ready to go home and cry! Well, what are we drinking to! To whatever happens next. Are you really going to trust someone who did a runner when things got tough? One beer, another, a double shot that spills when the glasses clink—just a few drops—in someone else's hand, a glass of wine, someone moves in with a soft drink. That's bad luck! Who ordered grape juice? This is a party, for fuck's sake, not a funeral. Grape juice. How old are you? Your mum let you go out all alone, sweetie? What a way to jinx the country! Should I get you another? One more toast! To us! What happened to solidarity? To us and to everyone else! To us, and to absent friends! To the bartender! Yes, that's right, to the bartender! Glass against glass against glass, a hand—hair on the knuckles, tips of the nails white, the leather strap of the wristwatch still looking brand new—joins in the toast from the group one table over; at the bar, it's hard to tell strangers apart from friends. María moves her toothpick—they weren't given forks—towards a plate of croquettes, aware that they belong to a group of men with moustaches, all of whom look the same: she can hardly distinguish between their hairstyles, their beards, their jackets; she skewers a croquette, and another later on, and another, until a fork that belongs to one of them taps on the dish, and when she looks up, he sees her chewing.

"It looks like we've got ourselves a thief!"

María begins to laugh nervously, her mouth still full of béchamel and bits of meat, and the guy looks at her and laughs too. He responds with what might be called ceremony: he makes a little bow before María, kisses her hand—the toothpick still in her closed fist, his saliva on her skin—asks the waitress to bring another round of croquettes, on him, for the lady, just for the lady. María says no, I couldn't possibly, I can pay, no problem; the bar smells of cigarettes, pickles, and sweat. The men in the group with the croquettes are smoking; now they're all watching her, her body turned towards her friends and her head towards them. She ends up turning around, as if at their request. They haven't requested anything, they've hardly said a word to her, but she has the strange feeling she owes them a little attention. She wasn't confused, really: maybe with the first croquette, thinking that Pedro had ordered them, but not with the second, when she'd already realized that the men next to her—their hands free of scars, their fingernails short and clean—were eating from that plate. Then she dared to have another, two more, as if with that action she were establishing a strange justice.

"Come on over, honey. Come and join us in a toast."

María observes the man who's speaking: the contrast between his hair—thick, black, and curly—and the thin moustache that seems to stretch the definition, a few sparse hairs on one side, a few on the other. And she tracks his gaze: the man is looking at her face, her body, and at her hands, as well. What he sees is cracked skin, peeling along the unpainted nails; what he's looking for, she imagines, is a ring. María has been here before, many times, and she knows how it ends, so she smiles and goes back to her group. She puts an arm around Pedro's waist and kisses his cheek. She hears the men's voices stepping all over each other, maybe some comment about her she can't quite make out. Here's a beer for you, María. I saw you finished the first one, you wanted another, right? We're celebrating today. It's a big day! Any of their friends would say the same. They agreed to meet up in a neighbourhood they hardly know: some of them work nearby and pass through it very early or very late; others have come down on the rare day off, like tourists in their own city. She doesn't remember who suggested it at the last meeting: if they win, we'll celebrate on Friday, right? Not on the day itself, since they can't take the time off work, but on Friday, no two ways about it. At a bar near the office, the boss decided we have to stay late to close out the month. What are you complaining about, mister minister, you're the only one here who wears a button-down every day! Another toast? Of course, to us! María came along because Pedro asked her to: if she hadn't, they wouldn't have seen each other until the week after, and anyway, she goes to all their meetings, and when the association needs someone to cook for seminars or clean after the occasional get-together, she always offers. It bothers some of them, they'd rather see each other without women or children, but someone asked who would do the mopping if not María, and they accepted it. If you down it, there's another round on me. Who ordered this glass of red? Come into a fortune, have you, kid? Who are you now, the Marquis of Slapdash Painter-Decorators? No, I'm Duke of the Nifty Gearsticks.

None of them is a member of any political party, though some like to think they're active in politics, in their way; others just enjoy the conversations, they make them feel like more than just grease monkeys. Pedro made an unforgettable speech about that one afternoon, sitting down with a plate of rice and vegetables: imagine the day when all of them—all the bosses and the bosses' bosses—realize we can actually think for ourselves. Some of them voted for the Spanish Socialist Workers' Party; others voted Communist—Pedro, María herself, and maybe one other friend, judging by the bitter look on his face when their eyes meet during one of the toasts, and by his conviction at the bar the week before when he expressed doubts about Felipe González's policies. María is sure this isn't a win for them, she told Pedro as much last night on the phone, but it's some consolation to see Pedro's friends—not her friends—so happy. She doesn't remember the first time she met any of them: she remembers meeting Pedro, of course, but not the first event one or another of them came to, or when they joined. Some had belonged to another group at a church nearby, which dissolved as soon as they changed priests; Pedro joined the neighbourhood association when his family situation became too much for him to handle alone. María gradually started going to meetings with him, because she had a lot of questions, and the upstairs neighbour went along, too; he'd helped Pedro negotiate his brother's benefits and thought he might be able to lend a hand with the bureaucracy.

To them, María is both constant presence and mere extension of Pedro. The group got into the habit of drawing out meetings at the bar on the corner near the association, and soon, they moved on to other topics: improving the paving on certain streets; volunteers to greet the widows, orphans, and folk with disabilities who came to fill out support requests; don't miss this book, this movie, this record. If they spent their days allowing their bosses to rage at them just to keep their jobs, how was fiction going to help them? It worked for some, others felt like impostors, others were unmoved but feigned enthusiasm so they wouldn't look bad in front of everyone else. There were also some who believed that all such things were a distraction from the real fight, and they insisted on doing more: becoming members of the party, unionizing, changing the world for real.

Some headed back to the neighbourhood that night, until there were four of them left: Alfonso, Víctor, Pedro, and María too. Víctor had burst into the bar shouting, "Tonight's the night!" and Pedro immediately ordered him a beer. His upper lip was now covered in foam: Víctor was always a little late in joining the group, and María came to see it as his way of ensuring himself a triumphant entrance, all eyes on him. He was the youngest, the most unworldly, and also the tallest. They'd given up playing jokes on him because he always fell for everything. His parents had come to the neighbourhood in the fifties from a village in Extremadura, and he was born after they were already settled in Carabanchel; this put him at a certain advantage in their meetings. Everyone knew he had played in those streets as a child, who would dare argue with him about what to do, how to behave.

"It's pretty incredible. A left-wing government, socialist, in our democracy. By absolute majority. Put there by the workers. This isn't a story people are going to forget."

"Earth to Víctor! Knock, knock!" Alfonso taps his knuckles against his friend's head. "Anybody home? Look at the paper. Here: 29th October 1982. They're already telling the story. The newspapers, the radio stations. Nobody's talking about anything else."

"Come on, we'll be yesterday's news before you can say Calvo-Sotelo! The only way future generations are going to find out about it is in books, in the movies. Same as it was for us."

"Yeah, but who's going to write them? You and me, we just got off work; sure, we get Sundays off, but you've got a family, Alfonso goes out to his in-laws', and I've got my own stuff to take care of. When do you think we're going to get to sit down and 'tell our story'? You know I can't write for shit. Even if I had the time, I wouldn't know where to start. I mean, if I had to get Juan José's help just for that thing with my brother…"

"Do you really think anyone's going to give a shit about what you've got to say, Pedro? They'll want to know what *these guys* have got to say—the bastards on the front pages. Forget about it, they're nothing like us. Like the fact they finished school. How many people our age do you know who managed that? And I don't mean Víctor's wife's little workshop. I'm talking about a proper education: university, all those years it takes, people's families paying their way for them. How many people our age do you know who actually managed that? And your bosses don't count. Juan José, if you actually stop and think, even he gets treated a little differently in the office. These guys here, the ones in the paper: these are our bosses."

"So they aren't on our side, Alfonso. That's what it means. They're the enemy."

"These guys and our bosses are the same, Pedro? Never. They're fighting the same fight as us. Fair pay, better hours, for our kids to have the same opportunities as everyone else. We've got to get behind them."

"In terms of what you said, Víctor, about somebody telling this story years down the line, it's that they'll be interested in what's happening here, in the photo, right? And in what happens with them. As for what we talked about here, in a bar, I don't think anyone will care. And even if they did, who would write about it? Are your kids going to, your grandkids? Do you remember that book we talked about last year? The one about the noble savage—*he* was a poor, ignorant worker, nice guy, struggled to put food on the table. Well that's exactly the same as us: where we come from, what our stories are, none of it matters. We play that same role, don't you get it?"

"I don't know, man, you've lost me. Are you trying to say my kids will be different from me?"

"More or less. If they study, if they go to university, they'll be different. If they make it out of the neighbourhood, get better jobs, then they'll have different lives. Right, Víctor?

Your wife, I know you sometimes go back to your home village, but she got out. Does she act like the women who stuck around? What does she say when she talks about them?"

"For fuck's sake, Pedro. It's Friday night. Can't you just drink and relax? Of course my wife's different from her cousins. She left, she came to Madrid. It's a whole other thing."

"That's just it: who writes for the papers? Who's up in Congress sounding off? If we do it like that, we'll be using the same language as our enemies."

"Again... D'you really think so? This story here, I read it, I can understand it. Look: Felipe González Márquez, forty years old, set, odds-on to become the new prime minister, affirmed this morning, in his first speech since the victory... I know you didn't go to university, I know you work at a hardware shop, but tell me, what out of all of that don't you understand? Me, it's those books you all talk about at the meetings, that what's I don't understand. You give them to me, I read them on the bus, but I'm buggered if any of it goes in. What *language* are they writing in? I'd like to see the hands of the people who wrote them: have they ever done a day's work with them, even once? I mean *work*: not picking up a pen or tippety-tapping away at a bloody typewriter. I don't know what language the enemy speaks, if the guys who are supposedly on my side don't even care if I understand what they're fighting for..."

"And who's the enemy? Those guys on the front page? OK, María. Help us out over here, will you? Pedro's getting upset. Come on, man, be a good sport."

Up until then, María has silently sat and watched: a sip of her beer, a slice of chorizo and bread, eating and drinking to wile away the time. She doesn't know if she should intervene, or rather, she knows she shouldn't: she doesn't want to make Pedro uncomfortable, and she doesn't want the others to sit there agape; it's no small feat to have got to join the outing rather than staying home. María's chosen silence, as always; she turns up at meetings and gatherings, writes down the titles of the books they mention and afterwards seeks them out to read, then transcribes the ideas in notebooks that accumulate on the shelf in the living room; but not once has she put her hand up. It's different at home: she talks about politics with Pedro, not so much what's happening now, but what will happen later. She thinks about the fact she has a daughter. Where will her daughter live? What will she have been through by the time she's María's age? In the examples she gives, however, she uses other people's children: what will life be like for Alfonso's kids, for Víctor's? Will they have to worry about making their mortgage payments, about having a beer at the bar on a Friday night? About how their story's told? When Pedro talks about ideas—not his own, but the ones she explains to him—in front of his friends, and she sees the way they respond, it makes María proud. It feels like a kind of recognition for her thoughts, although no one will ever know that she's the one thinking them.

"He just isn't as happy about it as everyone else. You have to understand... Pedro isn't convinced."

She looks around. Their discussion—which, after her intervention, becomes background noise—continues. She counts three women in the entire establishment: one of them, working between the kitchen and bar, around fifty, her apron covered in stains, she suspects is the owner's wife; another girl, very young, sits at a table with a group of boys around the same age—maybe twenty, students having something to eat before they go out—and her, thirty-three, forgoing hours of sleep to join in tonight's celebration. There aren't many women at the neighbourhood association, either, and she remembers that almost all of the ones who show up at meetings—herself included—go with their partners, and never say a word. The things she talks about with Pedro she tells the other women, too, one or two at a time: never too many at once, always in a living room, with a baby crying or a child playing at their feet. The atmosphere tonight reminds her of the first meetings she went to after she met Pedro, when he was still working at the factory with her cousin's husband, and heard him talking about worker solidarity one Sunday; from then on, she made sure to sit near him.

No one can know the truth about these women. Their enemy is the boss: the one with more money, more power, the one who changes their shifts without bothering to ask, who's always looking down on them. The boss is the enemy, and the boss's wife, and the boss's kid. But Loli once pointed out that the men who slept next to them were the enemy, too. We're here, she explained, telling everyone else we're just friends who meet up for coffee, who like to gossip about celebrity weddings, because our husbands wouldn't be able to stand hearing us out: they'd be the first to put an end to it. Conchita's youngest daughter saved pamphlets from university for them: divorce, abortion, feminism. How many kids have you had, Loli? Wouldn't you have rather suffered through one fewer pregnancy? Conchita, are you really going to wait for your husband to die to live on your own terms?

You're stronger and smarter than him, why should you have to stay home and take care of the kids when you could go out and earn your own money? The same goes for Irene, who worked the fields in the village—she's got some scars, and not all of them from the spade her brother taught her to use without telling their father—and is shut up at home now that they've come to the city, and if she decided to separate, what could she do to support herself? They've tried to help her, but they don't know how: there's no room in their homes for a woman and her children, and not even all their savings combined add up to enough for a small apartment or a divorce lawyer, and they don't say it out loud—María is ashamed of the feeling—but they don't want to risk becoming the target of her husband's rage either; they've heard too much about that from Irene. They don't talk about María's situation much, because it's hard for her. The women live on the same street, and they talk about that. Conchita's daughter patiently explains anything they don't understand; sometimes María stays with Loli's kids next door if she hears noises in the apartment; they all look out for Irene—as much as they can—who is the quietest. No one will ever know about the war they wage in their living rooms: imagine the day—María says one Saturday afternoon, more than just cream in her coffee, all of their husbands late coming home—when they realize we think for ourselves.

"But look at us"—María's voice—"We couldn't be at Calle Mayor or San Jerónimo yesterday because today we had to work. And today, instead of having beers at Matéo's in the neighbourhood, we've come to this place, I'm not really sure why. What are we trying to do? Pretend we're something we aren't? That group over there: they might be dressed like us, but they're lawyers. Their families put them through university. They live in nice apartments, close by. And those kids: they're students. What were you doing at nineteen, Víctor? What about you, Alfonso? Pedro? Were you out with your friends having beers on a Friday afternoon? Playing cards at some café? I was keeping quiet and cleaning up shit in one house or another, doesn't matter where, or who for. So what do you say now? Shall we all drink to the future?"

That's not what happened, of course. María pictured it, but then she kept quiet again, had a few sips of her beer, looked over the menu. Pedro asks if she's still hungry, because they're thinking of going to another bar, more music, fewer lights. Do you want to go home, María? Maybe you'd rather do that. She shakes her head no, no to everything: she isn't hungry, she doesn't want to go home. They pay, she says goodbye to the owner of the croquettes—he tries to meet her eyes, gives her a nod—and they go on to the next place.

"I like your trousers."

She hears the woman say she likes her trousers, but María is wearing leggings. It's the third bar of the night— the fourth, if you count the one where they had sharing plates and beers—and María thinks she's had too much to drink. It'll soon be time to convince Pedro that they ought to head back to the neighbourhood, have a quick shower, change clothes; tomorrow—now today—she'll work with a headache, but there remains the consolation of a rest in the evening, and Sunday off, although Pedro might want to come by for a while after lunch. When she agreed to meet up with them on Friday, she'd worked almost all of it out: a different sort of night, in a neighbourhood she hadn't set foot in since she moved to Madrid, one she only knew from newspaper clippings. There she is, in her black leggings and the shirt with the shoulder pads, so long that she thought it was a dress, in that bar where everyone seems to be four or five metres taller than her.

"I said I like your trousers."

"They're not trousers. They're leggings."

"So do you walk down the street with your arse out for all to see?"

No, she explains patiently, she has a knee-length coat, and the leggings are black—as I'm sure you can tell, she adds pointedly—and the shirt goes halfway down her thigh. In the end, she's translated into words what the woman could see if she troubled herself to look. María observes her: her dress is so short you can see her underwear; the fabric, shiny—I wouldn't dare wear a fabric like that, María thinks, not even on New Year's Eve—a pair of big, pineapple-shaped earrings, make-up she can tell is neon despite the low lighting in the bathroom. María barely put any make-up on, a little mascara and lipstick when they were already at the second bar. She hasn't had very much to drink after all, if she can describe the woman in such precise detail; or maybe she has, but she isn't a lightweight. That's what everyone says: María can drink like a man.

There's only one stall in the women's bathroom. A while ago, one girl came out, and another went in; she's taking a long time, and now there's a short queue. There's room enough for María and the other woman in the bathroom, and another girl stands outside and opens and closes the door to see what's happening. The other woman takes little sips of her beer, one after another, and chats away; María doesn't know if she's supposed to join in the conversation, or if the woman is just talking to fill a scary silence. From outside, the music seeps in, the voices, the sound of glass against glass.

"I'd rather have a beer than wine or a mixed drink. It makes me feel more present. Wine has its charm, that's for sure, but I pay for it afterwards. Does that happen to you? And mixed drinks, like sangria, say… they make me think of my dad and his friends, at parties in the summer. Not really my thing. I'd rather have a beer." She holds her bottle out towards Maria and mimes a toast.

"It's cheaper."

"I love your outfit, really. I said that already. Where's it from? Which shop? Wait, don't tell me: you didn't buy it here, did you? You got it on holiday somewhere. In London? Or the flea market, at least. Do you go to the flea market? Me, I only get records and fanzines there, nothing else."

The woman talks so quickly that she stumbles over her words. How old is she? María takes a good look: while she already has crow's feet, this woman barely does. But the fuchsia at the corners of her mouth droops a little, and that's the same as María. A little over thirty, then, like her? Thirty-three already, María thinks. How many kids did my mother have by my age? Her older brothers, for sure, and maybe her, too, if her maths isn't off. Not Soledad, and definitely not Chico. She thinks of her younger brother, whose shift must have ended a few hours ago; she likes the idea that maybe he's just finishing a movie. Would Chico want to be here with her? He stopped asking a while ago if he could come and visit her.

"Am I scaring you? Or boring you? My friends sometimes tell me I talk too much. They tell me to watch out for that. They're like, Lady, shut up."

She can't tell if Lady's making fun of her, if she's so drunk that there's no distinction any more between what she wants to say and what she should say, or if her thoughts simply run along like that—so fluidly—and all she has to do is let the words tumble out. She's finished her beer, and now she's raising the empty bottle to her lips. María finds Lady amusing. Her bag, her ankle boots, how much did they cost? Maybe enough to get María out of a tight spot one month, or to buy something nice for Carmen. A dress for Christmas, when she'll next go down to Córdoba. What size would she be now?

How tall is her daughter? She thinks that this is one way she can compensate for her absence; she thinks of gifts for the next holiday, Christmas, her birthday.

"Here all by yourself, girlie? Or are you with friends?"

"With friends."

"Are you guys in a group or something?"

"We met at a neighbourhood association in Carabanchel. I've been living there since I moved to Madrid. I hardly ever come over this way. They give classes, they have film and theatre groups. We talk about books, movies… Some of the neighbourhood kids belong to university film clubs, and we organize screenings with them. It's fun."

That last bit is lost, because halfway through María's reply, Lady's eyes are already creasing, followed by an exaggerated laugh. It's me, she thinks; she's laughing at me. It isn't the first time this has happened. María has learnt to pretend that she's vulnerable, naive, to say please—her voice soft, eyelids lowered slightly—would they mind repeating themselves, explaining what they mean, as if she didn't catch it the first time. Silly María, they'd say at the house she cleaned for a few years, where she gave her voice the high-pitched lilt she learnt from comedies. That's how María hardened herself against the likes of Lady.

"Those guys out there are going to help you. Those guys out there, all of them, they all voted PSOE. They're your guys."

The woman is slurring, she points her bottle, then her finger, in the direction of the door: draws an imaginary target, goes prattling on. The girl waiting on the other side of the door opens it, fuck this, she asks if the stall is still occupied, are you fucking kidding me, she pounds on the door a few times—first with her fist, then her right leg—bitch, I'm going to piss myself, and she leaves. A voice inside the stall asks for a few more minutes, Lady asks if she's OK, the voice says yes, she just needs a little more time, a minute or two. Lady says no problem at all and steps back, takes another sip from her empty bottle. María finds that she feels comforted by being shut up in the bathroom with Lady and the silent girl in the stall.

"I didn't vote PSOE. I voted Communist."

"Don't tell my friends, but me too. The Communists! If my father found out… We're a couple of losers, you know that? The party we voted for is in free fall. My grandmother was scared of them, but there's something about them I like. Equality for all! Look at us, you and me, the girl in the stall. All of us at the same bar, at the same time, all of us drunk. And what do we have in common? Hey, pisser! What have we got in common, you and me?"

While the voice asks again for a little more time, Lady takes María's hand, and they turn to look at themselves in the mirror. One woman's body alongside another woman's body: Lady's slim, muscled calves aren't so different from María's, a little wider, but sturdy, too; María's thighs are more generous, and her hips are wide, but her body tapers at the waist. Lady is more angular. If Lady lifted her dress, if María lifted her shirt, they would see the same stretch marks across their stomachs, and on Lady's, the scar from the C-section. One's chest is tiny—a pair of bee stings you could hardly even suck on, in the words of an ex during a break-up—and the other's the complete opposite. And the same features, in each face, how completely different they are: a mouth, a nose, two eyes. Lady's are open, and María's are closed. Lady goes on talking: incessantly.

"When I asked if you were in some kind of group, I meant a band. A musical group: this time of night, at this bar, everyone's in a band. I wasn't laughing at you. I'm an actress, I've been an extra in a couple of movies—dancing at a party, chatting in a place like this. That kind of thing. I'm too old for a band. But you're not. How old are you, little girl? I'm twenty-seven."

"I'm thirty-three."

"You don't look that old… You look like you could be twenty. Now I've told you all about myself. Your turn."

She holds out her hand, and María squeezes it. It's the second time in as many minutes that she's felt Lady's hand in hers, and she thinks the woman is right: the two of them have nothing in common. María really should head home soon, try to avoid getting light-headed in the morning, from the smell of the bleach. This weekend she'll rest, maybe tomorrow she'll call her mother so she can talk to her daughter.

"Do you know anyone who works in an office? I clean an office building. Every morning, I go in a couple hours before the first worker gets there. At seven, I'll be cleaning whatever they got dirty yesterday, so on Monday no one complains about spots on the carpet or cigarette butts in the ashtrays. Friday, Saturday: those days are the worst."

"I didn't know people did that."

"You wouldn't believe it… There are all kinds. The typist on the second floor always leaves us notes: thank you, have a nice day, I spilt my coffee and tried to clean it up myself. But that almost never happens."

"I meant you. People like you. You know what I mean? I never thought about someone coming to pick up the rubbish. I mean, I've seen you guys out on the street. But I've never talked to anyone like you."

They can hear the sound of urine in the background, a strong stream, unbroken, then the girl in the stall sneezes and stops, then the sound of the toilet flushing. The door opens, and a girl dressed just like Lady appears: the dress, extremely short and shiny; the backcombed hair—hers is brown; black eyeshadow on her eyes; chains around her neck and shoulders. Lady reacts; she opens her bag and takes out her purse. It's her turn. She looks for a note, and out from between bits of paper and credit cards, a photo falls to the floor. María bends to pick it up, and she looks—a knee-jerk reaction—at the face of the little girl: the same large, honey-coloured eyes as Lady, looking out from a round face. She tries to determine which features belong to the father—the pointy chin, the upturned nose—and which are from Lady. The hair colour she isn't sure about because Lady has dyed hers; she would bet that it's a light brown, given the shade of her eyebrows. If that's the case, then the girl also has Lady's hair, straight, in pigtails. In the photograph, the girl is putting on a smile, teeth clenched tight together.

"Look, girlie! It's my daughter. She's seven. I divorced her dad as soon as they made it legal. He wanted it just as much as I did. She's with my mother-in-law right now, she watches her for me some nights. You get it, don't you? I have to get on with my life. I meet a lot of people out, too. I never know when I'm going to land some role. And all that stuff about super-devoted mothers, sure, that's great, but not right now. I have to live my life while I can. Do you have kids?"

"Yeah, I have a daughter."

"Is she with your mother-in-law?"

"No, with my mum. About the same age as yours."

"Being a young mum isn't so bad. When she has her daughter, I'll be able to take care of her. I'll be a modern grandmother. You'll be the best grandmother in Carabanchel. Look at her, just look at her." The woman kisses the photo a few times, holds it up to María's face. "Smart and beautiful, too. She's little, but you can tell already: she cries until we give her what she wants. Do you have a picture of yours?"

"No. Not on me, I mean. At home, I do. Of course."

That's another way María and Lady are different. Two legs, two arms, a mouth, a nose, two eyes, a belly that carried a child: they have all of that in common, but not the lie María told about Carmen's age, not their ways of getting home—a taxi for Lady, maybe a friend's car, and the night bus for María—nor how quickly María will have to shower and leave for work, the conversations Lady will have all the way through to midday tomorrow. They don't both have a living room, or the room Lady set aside for her daughter, or the photographs of Carmen that María keeps tucked away. She put it in a drawer the first time Pedro came over: they started chatting at her cousin's every Sunday, and María said something about a dodgy appliance—the washing machine or the fridge, she doesn't remember now—and Pedro offered to take a look. María put away the first photo they sent her of Carmen, the one she'd hung up at her aunt and uncle's house, and the rest of the pictures from over the years: Carmen at the bar, Chico carrying her in a soft drinks crate, and Carmen in Soledad's arms at the neighbourhood fiesta. There were others, which Chico had framed and hung up in the bedroom that they had once shared and that now belonged to Carmen: they were of her and María, the mother observing her daughter with what from the outside might have seemed like tenderness, but from where she was standing—stretch-marks and all—it was those two small black eyes she saw, a record of the father. All the photos hidden, for the last eight years, in the bottom drawer of the TV stand. Pedro knows Carmen exists, of course, but she hasn't shown him a single photograph in all this time, hasn't even described her daughter's eyes, her nose, her mouth, her two arms and legs.

"My turn. Want to come too?"

María shakes her head and waits for Lady to go in, she takes a while and asks for another minute or two, like the silent brunette. It happens like this: the girl who was waiting opens the door again, comes into the bathroom, lines up next to María and mutters thank God, it's so hard to piss in these bars, I can't hold it for hours and hours, one beer after another, there's just no way, you have to tell me your secret. María closes her eyes, stops listening, and would swear that she even falls asleep for a minute or two. She wakes up to a tap on the shoulder: Lady is shaking her gently, while she touches up her make-up and tells her it's her turn. María does the maths again and thinks she and Pedro should have left a while ago. She starts to lift her shirt up while she opens the bathroom door, and turns around before pulling down her leggings:

"You didn't ask, but my name's María."

"Lady. It's Asun, really, but I didn't think it was... *enough.* You know what I mean? Everyone calls me Lady."

Crouching so she doesn't touch the toilet seat, eyes closed because it improves her aim, she pisses out the night's beer. She hears Lady talking to the girl who's still waiting: they reproach themselves for all the time they've wasted in the bathroom, then end up realizing they know each other, friends in common. María looks for a tissue in her handbag and wipes with it. When she comes out, Lady is gone, the girl who was waiting is still waiting, and the one from the dance floor is back, too.

"That took you a while, didn't it?"

"You're telling me… There was a queue. We ought to be heading home already."

Wearing cheap clothes, smelling of petrol and ammonia, what do Pedro and his friends think they're doing? Who do they think they are? Lady's group crashes into her field of vision, then the quiet girl's group, then the friends of the girl who was waiting in line behind her. She looks at them, all of them still deep in conversation. María closes her eyes, walks a few metres away to dance on her own, she has the feeling that some of the guys from the first bar are closing in on her at this last one, goes back and takes Pedro's hand. Felipe González prepares for the transfer of power with Calvo Sotelo; the Revolutionary Council of Portugal disbands; the Olivetti Electric, hit one key and a whole page comes out: the headlines of the newspapers that will go out to the kiosks a few short hours from now. She doesn't know, because she's drinking and drinking and dancing a little, sometimes holding Pedro's hand—he stays where he is—and sometimes breaking away from him. Do the newspapers speak of her, eyes, nose, mouth, legs, arms, the traces on her body of the mother she isn't? Do power and revolution speak of her? Glass against glass against glass, three hands—hair on the knuckles, blackened fingernails, worn wrist straps on their watches—and a hand—knuckles smooth, nails trimmed short, a thin silver bracelet on the wrist—to the lady of the group! Yes, that's right, cheers to the girl who's here with us tonight! Here you go, María: have another. Why? Why did you order another round? What are we drinking to? An empty bottle, two half-empty ones, someone just ordered another: we have to leave now, or this one won't make it to work, you're going to make me wait for her to change, my wife'll kill me if she wakes up and sees I'm not back yet. The cold trace of a bottle on the others' fingers. One more toast! Don't cry, María, we're leaving right now, I'll drink it quick, and we'll get you back home in no time, you don't have to shower, just fix your hair, and I'll take you to work, stop crying, María, please. To us! To us and everyone else! To the girl who's with us tonight! Yes, that's right, to her!

THE DREAM

Madrid, 2008

"I'VE DREAMT ABOUT MY FATHER's suicide every night since I was thirteen. I'm going to fall asleep soon, and I want to tell you about it now, because tomorrow this is how I'll wake: having just seen my father hanging from a tree. Don't be scared: I don't talk in my sleep, I won't burst into tears when the alarm goes off; I'm used to it now. Some men have told me I snore, others that I toss and turn; what happens for me is that every night, my father crashes his car—intentionally—but when that doesn't do the job, he goes and hangs himself from a tree instead. They probably already told you. It's always the same: they say my name, my age, maybe where I'm from or what I do, if I'm working at the time, and then they lower their voices and say my dad killed himself. It's like they're feigning a hurt they can't feel; they didn't know him, and they don't know the circumstances, either, or the reasons he did what he did. Or maybe it's pity that makes them lower their voices: maybe they see me as victim of the moment my father killed himself, of everything that set in motion, and any wrong move I make, they trace back to that decision of his. For years, I took a kind of comfort in that: my father's suicide gave me carte blanche to do whatever I wanted, with the pain and grief of it all as my excuse. But the truth is, even before it happened I liked being cruel, even as a kid. I mean, I took pleasure in it. I couldn't, I can't help it, to this day: I enjoyed making fun of classmates who didn't have as much money as me, or who weren't as clever. Back then that was pretty easy, and it didn't bother me when I got left out of all the playground games, or when I didn't get invited to their birthday parties. They also probably told you I'm not a very good person. Your friend must have warned you, at least. I have a younger sister. No, we hardly ever talk. I'll tell you about it another time. Eva, her name is Eva, she's four years younger than me, and we've always been complete opposites: she's incredibly outgoing, she used to love spending the weekend at one of our father's restaurants, running from table to table and playing waitress. When my father died, Eva went deep inside herself, she hardly spoke, but she would draw all the time; that was her way of expressing herself, not that I know, or really care, what she was trying to say. My mother was raised by an aunt and uncle of hers, and it always seemed strange to me that before the suicide, my sister was so much like him, like Chico, and after, she turned into a carbon copy of Aunt Soledad—such an apt name, she's the most solitary woman I know. Eva always got by on imitation, mimicking whichever behaviour made her feel safest. It could be that she doesn't have much of a personality: she's my sister, but I don't really know her. I've never been that interested in her life, not back then, and not now. I already told you we barely speak. I think what happened with my father changed Eva. Not me. I was like this already.

"But the dream, I was talking about the dream. Initially, I always woke up the way people do in the movies: back of my neck bathed in sweat, and aware I'd just cried out. It's the same every time: the car crashes into the tree, he gets out, shaking all over, he makes a noose from the seatbelts, and he hangs himself from the tree. You'll think it's strange, but I've learnt to control it: not the dream itself, really, but the space I occupy, the role I play. It's weird, because they say dreams take place in the unconscious, we're not supposed to have any control over them: but in the dream, my perspective changes every night, sometimes I see the suicide from across the road, and others, I'm in the passenger seat; sometimes I even think about giving him a boost so he can reach the noose more easily, die more quickly. Most of the time, though, I'm far away enough that he doesn't realize I'm there, too far away to really do anything. Are you following the metaphors? Yeah, metaphors. Like riddles: you allude to something, you explain it without stating it outright. Something like that. Though I really couldn't care less about literature, I see that the reason I never do anything in the dream, why I haven't once, not since I was thirteen years old, is that nothing I could have done would have changed his mind. I hide in the trees: it's a metaphor.

"These last few weeks, something bizarre has been happening: my father doesn't show his face. It's not every night; some of the time, the dream happens exactly the same as it has all these years. But some nights—and not because anything special's happened, all my days are exactly alike—I know it's my father because I recognize his broad shoulders, that back of his, and because I'm already waiting for the noose to go up, but still he doesn't show his face. And the face I see just before I wake, the crusted blood, the closed eyes, is my own. It hadn't happened for almost ten years: it happened once, just once, my first year of secondary school. The first night—no, not the first, the second—I woke up in complete shock, I could barely breathe, feeling the same way I had at thirteen, back when the dreams still had that effect on me. I thought it was just something my head was doing on its own: maybe from time to time it would add a new element into the dream to stop me from getting bored, to stop me from relaxing. I didn't give it very much thought. But I've dreamt that version a few times now, it's no longer the exception, and I actually find it funny, because I have none of my father's features. I look much more like my mother's side. Not like my mother herself, except for these rat eyes we both have, but like her aunt and uncle, absolutely, physically speaking. I guess like my grandmother, too, or at least that's what they tell me. I've never met her. She had my mother, visited her a few times when she was little, and disappeared. I think she lives in Madrid, too."

Her father's body swinging side to side, hanging from a noose and from a branch; her father's corpse waiting for some strangers to come along, their compensation a story they'll be able to tell forever and ever. One summer afternoon, poolside: I never told you about that day when my parents and I were on our way back from one of the steak houses in the mountains, did I, or years later, in the TV room at the nursing home: and then my husband parked the car as best he could and went to see if it was a body or just a prank someone was pulling. Their mother decided that Eva was too little to go to the funeral, and she stayed home with Aunt Soledad; but Alicia had to sit right at the front, receiving the condolences of people she'd never met who would vanish from their lives as soon as the mass was over. Also that summer: the apartment they were living in sold more quickly than they thought it would, and Alicia had no trouble putting her doll collection in a rubbish bag, although her mother had offered to keep them in a box until they moved into the new place. Those toys belonged to another life; it didn't make much sense to save them.

Alicia spent the summer at Uncle Chico's place, sometimes going to the pool at the sports complex with Eva and their aunt, feelings beginning to settle as the weeks went by, watching one movie after another without anyone bothering her. All her uncle's movies starred beautiful women with long blond hair, and chain-smoking men who came along to deliver them from sin. There were also women who held on to their character, and women whom life did not treat particularly well. Alicia asked her uncle which one she should watch the next day every time he got back from the restaurant, and he would get so excited talking about them they'd end up watching together. When the title card saying "The End" appeared, he would ask what she thought of it, who her favourite character was, if she found the ending convincing. That summer, Uncle Chico's face thinned, and he suddenly became half the man he had been.

Alicia managed to forget what happened in the years that followed, and this—in a sense—is the voice of her memory.

She thinks of that phase as a long transition from her previous life to her present one: purgatory, the space between heaven and hell, though she isn't sure which is which. After what happened in her first year, her mother requested a transfer to the secondary school in their new neighbourhood in Córdoba, the same neighbourhood where they'd been living when she was born, and there, Alicia bumped into some kids she'd known in primary; she pretended she didn't know them. She never talked about her family, though everyone already knew who she was, and she focused on her studies. The counsellor said she was proud of her: she'd gone from repeating year six to top marks in every subject. Alicia didn't enjoy it, but it kept her occupied, just like the movies. First, Uncle Chico lent her his membership card for the video shop, and later, Alicia learnt to download them. She didn't enjoy it—she never confessed—but it kept her occupied; reading demanded effort, and with movies, the stories took place right before her eyes, they required nothing of her. She passed exam after exam, chose the humanities over the sciences; Uncle Chico was proud when she settled on audiovisual communications. It wasn't too hard to justify to her mother, who knew how voraciously she consumed films, and it guaranteed that she would have to leave the city. Seville and Malaga were too close by for Alicia; at that distance, she'd be expected to go home every weekend. She chose Madrid. Her mother cried, just the way she was supposed to. That's how she treated her all those years: the way a mother was supposed to treat a daughter. She congratulated her on her marks every term, while Eva stopped talking, got held back, skipped class, announced that she had no interest in wasting her life at school. Alicia's mother told her how to get men to respect her, how to keep from getting pregnant too young—Alicia had to admit it was ironic—and worried when she stayed home on Saturdays or refused to go on the end-of-year trip. She imagined her mother making a list, noting down steps and crossing them out—"today, show that I'm understanding," "tomorrow, take an interest in her future plans"—before she went to bed.

Alicia did resemble her in that way. Uncle Chico often said so, laughing: Carmen didn't have much of a sense of humour, not even when she was little, but boy, was she clever, and he would tell stories about the days when he and Aunt Soledad shared a bedroom with the crib, the strange feeling of becoming a grown man alongside a growing girl. Alicia has never had a sense of humour, but she has always been clever: she figured out what to study so she could escape with no questions asked, and she worked out a way to support herself without her mother's help. Between the scholarship and the benefits for children with a deceased parent, she would be able to afford a room in halls, feed herself, pay her tuition. After everything that had happened, Alicia had managed to re-establish order, to shift her life back onto the path they had pulled her from. It wouldn't be too hard for her to get back what was rightfully hers. In a few years, she would have her degree, and then she could get a good job, pay for her own apartment, go on a real holiday or two, maybe even send some money to her family.

That's not what happened. Alicia moved into an apartment with two girls she knew from secondary school because their mothers were looking for someone for them to share with, and they got Carmen to agree to it, and she had no other choice; everything cost double what she had calculated, and soon, it wasn't just her mother she was calling every week, but Uncle Chico, too, inventing supposed materials for courses that didn't exist, asking him for money. She found her classes boring, and she didn't fit in with her classmates: their general enthusiasm pushed Alicia out of the conversation. She thought the way they talked about movies was ridiculous, these kids without the money for real film school or the talent to pass the entrance exams. They joked that she was a cynic—again, she had to acknowledge the humour: if only they knew—because she'd explained that she just wanted to make money and didn't care much, if at all, about art. She stopped going to her classes: not overnight, but skipping one class here, another there, not showing up at exams, or racking up so many absences that they wouldn't let her sit them. She thought about enrolling in a degree that would feed into the public sector later, maybe law, or maybe she could teach. Language and literature? She was good at analysing sentences—all that language stuff, it's so strange the way words affect people—and reading wasn't so hard. But in the meantime, she had to support herself, and she looked for her first jobs: waiting tables at a café in Argüelles for a few hours, then a full shift behind the bar, and half a year passed that way, and she decided to look for another shared apartment, where none of her flatmates would be calling her mother's neighbours and telling them about her apathy. She didn't enjoy the work—who enjoys being on their feet all day long, serving one coffee after another, making sure that table doesn't leave without paying first, and the other gets the right change—but she needed it. She didn't have to think much, and she was earning a wage to boot. She stopped asking Uncle Chico for money. She did talk to him sometimes, every two or three weeks; the calls with her mother turned into emails to Eva, which both of them could read. No one complained.

All these years, going from one job to the next, Alicia has taken the green line south, past the river: the café, a clothes shop, Puerta de Toledo, Pirámides, another café, a bingo hall, Marqués de Vadillo, several months of unemployment, Aluche, a cleaning company, Urgel, a supermarket, Eugenia de Montijo. The uniform suits her, and now she's living alone for the first time: a little apartment she rents from a co-worker. The lady of the house died there, washing dishes in the kitchen, and not a week had passed before Alicia was hanging up her clothes in the wardrobe, eating breakfast a few floor tiles away from the place where she may have pressed her hand to her chest, trying to reactivate her heart. The neighbourhood doesn't seem too bad to her, and just in case, she puts aside what money she can: she pays attention to offers on food approaching its sell-by date, so she can get to them before anyone else. She makes the most of the tap water: half a glass in the microwave to reheat rice without it going dry, the pasta soaking thirty minutes before she cooks it to hide the fact it's the cheap brand. Alicia doesn't enjoy her life, but her life keeps her occupied.

"The thing with my dad? At first, they told us there'd been a car accident. Not long after, I found out that was exactly what they were saying in the neighbourhood, and I guess my uncle or my mother, I don't remember which, decided to take advantage of the rumours: they told us my father had gone up into the hills to visit one of the steak houses, because he was thinking of buying it, and on his way back, he lost control on a bend, and he crashed. My father owned a bunch of restaurants. He started out as a waiter, working with my Uncle Chico, who's actually my mum's uncle, not mine, and who isn't really an uncle to me—he's some strange combination of father and mother, maybe. As a teenager, my mother would sometimes stop by when Chico was working, on her way out of the city centre, and they'd make their way back to the neighbourhood together. My father was a little older than her, not by much, just five or six years, and my mother got pregnant right away, even younger than my grandmother had been, and it was very much a shotgun wedding. By the time I was born, they'd moved in with my Uncle Chico. He had a little apartment in the neighbourhood—still lives there—with a nook which is only for watching movies, because he loves film. Her grandparents couldn't bear watching my mother repeat their daughter's story, they wanted nothing to do with her; one aunt was already living with her husband and children at my other grandparents' house, on my father's side, and they didn't have any more room. So while my parents were looking for a place to live, trying to save a little money, Uncle Chico turned his bedroom over to them, and took the movie room for himself, that pallet where I've slept so many times since. I talk about him a lot because he's been really important to me. He chose my sister's name. My name's Alicia. My father chose it.

"My father took his new role as head of the household seriously, and he got a job waiting tables at a restaurant where he made a little more money, and I didn't see him much after that, because by the time he got home I'd already have been asleep for hours. I honestly barely remember him. I've filled in this story with the things Uncle Chico would tell me, and what I heard him say to my mother, or Aunt Soledad; the things my mother says, or said, have always seemed more like lies than the truth. My mother's very smart; beautiful, I don't know, I guess maybe when she was younger, but I have no idea any more, we haven't seen each other in years. I'll tell you about that later. First they bought an apartment, then my father opened his first restaurant, and Uncle Chico ran it with him. It did pretty well, and when Eva was born, my parents bought another apartment, in a better neighbourhood, closer to the city centre. My father opened four restaurants in ten years, all in nearby neighbourhoods: Carmen's, it was called, Carmen numbers one, two, three, and four, though Carmen—my mother—hardly ever set foot in them. When my father killed himself, he had just opened the fifth, right in the centre, and he'd bought another apartment, in one of those new buildings with a pool, right by the school we'd be going to the following year. You could say they'd done well for themselves: my Uncle Chico learnt to walk before the neighbourhood had street lights, and when my father was born in that same neighbourhood, there weren't even sewers yet. That's what they came from, and that's what they left behind, and every restaurant and apartment they bought was bigger than the last, and in a nicer neighbourhood: they hadn't had much chance to study, but we would, at a private school, and we'd share desks with other people like us. My mother didn't care to run into the neighbours at the supermarket near our building, so she drove to El Corte Inglés and did the shopping there; she did the same thing with clothes and appliances, all of it charged on a credit card. Eva had no idea what was going on, she was happy just doing her little dances at break time, but I was a living embodiment of my mother's disdain, in a way; I was shameless, to the point of boastfulness: in class, I was aware that I was better than the other girls around me. I had to repeat the last year of primary school, because I knew that whether I passed or not, I would have a better life than the rest of them; their clothes were so cheap and ugly, the same tracksuits every time we had PE, the knees of their jeans patched up. What did I want to be back then? I don't really know. If all that had never happened, I guess I might have studied business, and my father would have set me up in an office next to his, and a few years after that, I would have married someone I met at university and stopped working, or popped into the office once or twice a week. But the reality is, my father killed himself: a dream reminds me every night of my life. Like a warning that startles me into accepting the life I've lost, and also accepting the one I'm living now."

When the girl from work introduced him to her, she didn't quite catch the first part of the word; she was left with, at most, the final thrust of the name. She didn't find him attractive: too tall and hawk-nosed, with bulging eyes. Nor was she all that interested in the conversation: on weekends, he rides his

bike, he joined a cycling club as soon as he finished secondary school, and he insists on describing the early mornings,
the routes they take on Saturdays and Sundays, in full. The
slopes, the sights, how long has he been talking about all
this? Fifteen minutes, an hour; Alicia is good at pretending
to listen, at feigning interest, but really she's thinking how
lucky she is to have tomorrow off. She thought he said he
lives in Canillejas—now, already back at his apartment,
it's confirmed—and he asks where she lives. Alicia almost
always lies, invents a name and a job and a neighbourhood,
but he knows her co-worker—it's Rocío's birthday—and he
would have found her out soon enough. That Alicia lives
in Eugenia de Montijo, the final stop at the far end of the
same metro line, seems like a sign to him; to her, it's a bad
joke. He bought the apartment a few years ago, planning
to marry the woman he was with at the time, but she left
him, and now he lives alone. He got stuck in the loop that
so discomfits Alicia—admiration for the girl he fell in love
with, his dismay when she ended things, blatant resentment
of the woman who left him—and she noticed that on several
occasions he said "girlfriend" instead of "ex-girlfriend," as if
she had fled two weeks ago and not a year. She had tried to
make eye contact with one of her co-workers, so she could
go and join them, break free of him, but they all ignored her.

Then Alicia tried to bring herself to imagine his naked
body—beer belly, tan lines on his calves—and was repelled;
she felt a chill of pure disgust run up and down her spine. He
noticed; he noticed that her eyes closed and her shoulders
shook, and he asked if she was cold, if she wanted a jacket.
Alicia can't deny that in that moment—not the moment of

cheap gallantry, but the moment when she imagined his naked body—everything changed: she thought his voice sounded nicer, and she looked at his thin upper lip and his brimming bottom one and accepted the fact that if he decided to kiss her, she wouldn't pull away. She re-entered the conversation: he was asking about the supermarket, and she said the shifts were reasonable, and she and the other staff got on. He said nothing to this: maybe he was waiting for Alicia to continue, or, since he'd droned on for ages—his passion for cycling, the separation, the thrilling life of a single man in his early thirties—for her to introduce a topic. She said to herself, Alicia, if you want something, you have to give something up in return. Here we go.

"Do you like movies?"

"Oh, I'm not a huge fan. I'm not much of an intellectual."

"Not all movies are for intellectuals…"

"But you don't really seem like one either. Am I right?"

"Why? Because I work at a supermarket?"

He came closer. A tiny step, and there was even less distance between the upper part of his body and hers. Alicia was about to change her mind, to take advantage of that last remaining metre: but she liked thinking about what would happen afterwards, about that body she imagined looked ridiculous on a bike. Surely he had photos at home of his friends from the cycling club. What would it take for him to show them to Alicia? She thought maybe when they went inside and he offered her a drink, she could ask. Have you won any races? Do you have a trophy, a medal? Maybe a group photo. I've never met anyone in a cycling club. He had told Alicia all about his friends and their absurd nicknames, and she couldn't stop thinking about those bodies stuffed into cycling shorts, the jerseys that barely zipped up. How much had he spent on that gear? Had his ex-girlfriend bought some of it for him, maybe on the last birthday they were together? Alicia said yes, but she would never know what the question had been; he leant towards her, and she told him no, not in front of everyone else, that's embarrassing. He offered to pay for a taxi, and they left the bar together. When they turned the corner, he kissed her.

Alicia discovered sex when she left home. In secondary school, she hadn't so much as kissed anyone; she hated women and didn't like any of the boys she knew. She may have been slightly attracted to some of her classmates, but only the ones she wouldn't have dared mention to a friend—not that she had any of those either: Miguelín, who stuttered, or Juan Antonio López, who you could tell apart from Juan Antonio Pérez because one played basketball and the other— López—did nothing to hide his psoriasis. Miguelín improved with years of speech therapy, and López gradually learnt to look on the red, scaly patches with shame: that neutralized any interest. Alicia came to realize that the idea of physical problems appealed to her, and overwhelmed her in practice: the twenty-something in a wheelchair who ate lunch at the restaurant with his family every Sunday and whose legs had been amputated below the knee, the boy in the classroom one door down, with complex syndactyly of the fingers on his left hand: she noticed them but didn't imagine herself naked, in the same room as them, the leg that led not to a foot but a stump, the flipper trying to close around her breast. She observed the sex scenes in the movies she watched at a scientific distance, to figure out what was happening, and not once did she try to masturbate. She wasn't interested in pleasure, or at least not in the kind the body supplied.

Alicia knew who Diego was because they'd taken a few classes together; she never found out how old he was, but she knew he'd enrolled after years spent working odd jobs, and that his work schedule at the time could only accommodate a couple of classes. When he spoke in class, he stood out for his limited vocabulary, for the clumsiness of his arguments: he didn't want to impose his opinion or show his maturity, only to justify his presence there, so he could feel like an equal instead of an intruder. Soon, he had two or three friends to buy beers and discuss directors with, always referring to them by their last name, in a low voice, as if he were keeping a secret. Alicia felt sorry for Diego, she found him ridiculous.

When Diego—with his notebooks and papers laid out in the second row—raised his hand, Alicia noticed her heart beating faster. She took pleasure in the film lecturer's tone when she responded, annoyed that she'd been interrupted by Diego, and began to look forward to Friday afternoons, when Diego made a fool of himself with each and every comment. While the lecturer dismantled his arguments point by point, Alicia looked at his thinning hair, the worn-out fabric of his checked shirt. One day, riding the metro to class, she surprised herself thinking of ways to approach him. Join up with the group he went out with every Friday? Too boring, too many people, hardly intimate. Flatter him: that would work. Over the course of several weeks, Alicia noted down each reference he made: last names of directors she researched and found out weren't as obscure as he made them out to be; she had seen a lot of their films, thanks to her uncle. Diego was reading Carver and listening to Springsteen, so Alicia read Carver—she took one of his books out at the library—and listened to Springsteen.

It took Alicia just a few conversations—that first afternoon: hey, what did you say the name of that director was, the one who also writes, from Brooklyn?; and the week after that, beaming: I watched the movie you recommended, I loved it—for Diego to decide he'd rather have drinks with Alicia and ditch the boys from film club. Alicia paid attention to Diego's every move as he sipped his beer, to apply them to future encounters—interests: cinema, above all else; dreams: live in New York City, direct a film; an insecure display of knowledge: telling her all about the filmographies she already knew by heart; a reference to some girl so she'd know that her forming part of his *mise-en-scène* was more the norm than the exception. Diego never talked about his job, but he did say he lived in an apartment that had belonged to his mother, and that his mother had moved back to the village years ago. Later, Diego fulfilled his promise: he kissed her on the third beer, and Alicia felt his tongue enter her mouth, and with it, bits of tortilla, chorizo, and bread soaked in oil, and Alicia wasn't disgusted but instead thought he fed himself like a baby bird. Diego took her to his apartment on the back of his moped—he lent her his helmet—and they fucked on a maroon imitation-leather sofa, crocheted rugs on the floor. Alicia didn't bleed. He hardly took five minutes to finish; she kept an eye on the DVD player display. She got up early, and he offered her a ride home, the proper thing to do. When they said goodbye, he kissed her neck. Alicia didn't go back to film history or communication theory, but she did learn where to find pleasure.

How many men like Diego has she slept with in the years since? One night, then the next: friends of her co-workers, some of her co-workers too; strangers she met at the bar below her apartment, or getting off the metro. She was fond of forty-something divorcees, too young to give in to solitude, but mortified when it came to undressing in front a stranger. While she flirted with them—always the same way: she would act shy, let them feel powerful, in control—she imagined them asking forgiveness if they couldn't get it up, if they came too soon. If she could avoid it, she didn't stay the night; she went home, showered, had something to eat, watched TV for a while, and went to bed. When she closed her eyes, Alicia was once more presented with the sight of her father's limping body.

"At first, they told us there had been an accident, but not even two weeks later, I overheard my mother talking to my uncle. The sympathy calls of those first few days had quickly turned into calls from the lenders: the manager of one bank branch wanted to know how we were going to pay for the new apartment, the manager of another was asking about the loan for the refurb at the new restaurant, the meat supplier was complaining that nobody at any of the restaurants was telling him anything, the creditors were on edge. My father's business had taken on debt after debt, not just loans, but favours, too, and that was the basis of our entire way of life. The apartments, the trips, the TVs, they weren't paid for by the dish of the day or the family-friendly atmosphere, but by my father's flawed financial logic; he was convinced he could cover up one failing business by taking over another. When no bank would approve any more loans and the creditors started demanding their money, my father had the brilliant idea of swerving off the highway and pretending his death was an accident; he thought the life insurance would fix everything. But he didn't manage it the first time, so failing even at that, he decided to hang himself.

"In that conversation, my mother talked, and Uncle Chico listened. She told him everything: the chaos in the accounts, the warnings, my father's complete ineptitude—first calls, then visits—while my aunt Soledad kept Eva and me busy at the pool. I was struck by the language she used to refer to him, the way she insulted someone whose body had been in the ground for less than a fortnight: to my mother, my father was a loser who'd left us stranded, a shit husband incapable of solving a single problem; I was amazed by the way she removed herself from the situation, her problems and his, some stranger hanging from a tree. My uncle would interrupt from time to time and ask her not to be so harsh, to try to understand, but my mother raised her voice, and she always found a way of saying something cutting. That's how I found out, and that's how I told Eva before I came to Madrid, after I passed the entrance exam. I gradually started packing up my things, I didn't have much, and I spent the rest of the summer at Uncle Chico's. I thought it was funny. The symbolism, I mean. The metaphors. Spending my last days in that city in the house where I'd spent the first days of my life.

"I have to admit, my mother made all the arrangements quickly and cleanly. She accepted her fall and went back to square one. It's the only thing I've ever admired about her: she held her head high while climbing out of that nouveau-riche costume. She sold the new apartment, and the one we were living in. We split up and stayed with some relatives, the ones we had relationships with—we knew nothing about my grandmother's older siblings—until the previous tenants left the little apartment. We went back to our old neighbour-hood, our real neighbourhood: the poor neighbourhood. The restaurants were closed, the apartments and one of the properties sold, which settled almost all of the debts, while the rest they started paying off little by little; when I left home, there was still a balance owed to some bank. My uncle kept the restaurant in our neighbourhood. And that's how my mother, Eva, and I ended up back in the lives we had tried so hard to escape. And they all lived happily ever after.

"I'm not telling you all of this because I want you to feel bad for me, and I'm not trying to paint some romantic picture of myself, either: a rich girl who woke up poor one day. I'm not interested in being sentimental. I miss my father, but I also miss something I never experienced, something I was entitled to: not having to go to work, opening a full fridge, holidays the people I now spend my time around could never afford. It's not really my father I miss, or that life, but the way I saw my father, and everything his death prevented. I miss the self-made man whose picture sometimes showed up in the paper, who paid generously for overtime, and whom all his employees admired, who left a tip even if he was just buying our schoolbooks. I'm jealous when things go well for people, and I take comfort in their troubles—they make me feel less alone. I don't want pity because I don't deserve it. And I don't want your pity, I hardly know you, I don't know your story, but you can tell me it if you want, I'll listen; I'd really rather leave your apartment right now, but to get back to mine, I'd have to take a few buses, the metro won't be open for an hour, and I don't have the money for a taxi. I'm trapped here, with you. Look: another metaphor. Uncle Chico's restaurant? Yeah, it's still open. My mother works in the kitchen, and I think my sister started helping out there a while back, too. It'll be another fifteen or twenty years before he gets to retire, and I guess at that point one of them will take over. He wanted to be a teacher, go back to school and get a degree, but he chose to carry the weight of the family instead. No one asked him to do it. I hope then he'll finally have some time for himself, time to rest. No, they never changed the name… They're still calling it Carmen's. What did you expect, the big finale, a happy ending? Life just isn't like that."

ABUNDANCE

Madrid, 1984

F ROM TUESDAY TO SATURDAY, her alarm goes off at
5.30 a.m.; Mondays, she gets an extra thirty, forty minutes, since she and Teresa have been in over the weekend to
empty the rubbish bins and air out the offices. Some days,
if the weather is good—if it's not raining, if the cold is still
bearable—she leaves home a little early and takes the bus,
even though it means buying another ticket. She changes
lines at Atocha and enjoys looking out at the different cities
that exist within the same city. Russian dolls: more than
neighbourhoods, cities within cities within cities, houses and
streets inside the belly of the same whale. María thinks about
the older buildings in her neighbourhood, and also about the
new ones, four or five storeys tall, with identical red-brick
facades and patterned awnings, extending towards the sky
once the bus is on the other side of the river and heading
for the train station. She thinks about the first association
meetings Pedro invited her to, about his friends and the
others demanding the neighbourhood be cleaned up, that
it become, they insisted, "dignified." What kind of a view
are we getting, they wondered: the jail, the shanty areas, the

empty lots; and María thought for the first time about the way people described the streets where she'd lived. When you cross the Manzanares on your way to the city centre, the buildings become more polished, the past alternates with the future. She thinks about her first weeks in Madrid, when the metro went only as far as Oporto and she walked from there to her aunt and uncle's place, and she thinks of the times when she got the lines mixed up, that time she ended up in Alfonso XIII and had so much trouble finding her way back home. Now she works in Nuevos Ministerios, and she takes the metro straight there if she's in a hurry. Since in that case her only view is of her fellow passengers' faces, she uses the time to read: Laura, Conchita's daughter, lends her lots of books and encourages her to join groups where she can discuss the things she cares about, the things Loli and Conchita care about, but surrounded by other women. I tried to get my mum to go, Laura tells her, but there's no way. Not for María, either: she worries they'll think she's strange, or worse, they'll make fun of her ignorance. As if the instant she opened her mouth, they'd know all about her, where she was from, how much money she made, and she would realize, with all those women looking on, that her opinion wasn't worth very much. Most of the books Laura lends her she's read about or heard about on the radio; every time Laura calls to tell her she'll be coming by the next afternoon, María feels conflicted. She appreciates Laura's efforts, that instead of staying at the library or having a drink with her friends, she goes over to María's, but she has the feeling she's becoming a kind of lab rat: María, the single, daughterless mother, the socially conscious office cleaner, educated by Laura, daughter of Domingo and Conchita, construction worker and housewife, the first in her family to set foot inside a university. She thought maybe Laura pitied her, or maybe she was trying to clear her conscience: every scholarship she got, every course she passed, took her further and further away from the neighbourhood. Maybe she hoped seeing María would anchor her in her surroundings—the place where she belonged, the place she was escaping from, though not without remorse—or that María would grab her by the ankles so she couldn't take off. What a sweet little fable.

She and Teresa split the offices, and María looks them all over before the managers clock in; later on—when they've started up with the typewriters and meetings, and the news is on in the background—they take care of the common areas. She likes working with Teresa, because they have a way of chatting that doesn't spill over into prying: sometimes she'll mention Pedro or her conversations with Chico, but she avoids talking about Carmen; she knows Teresa was born in a village in Granada, that she lives in Colmenar, and that she's getting married for the second time in February, though she thinks it's a horrible month. María also likes to work. When the metro passes through Sainz de Baranda and Conde de Casal, she overhears other women complaining about the smell of the floor cleaner, the cracks in their hands; her hands hurt, too, but she takes a certain pride in the cleanliness. Over time she has learnt to appreciate her role: tidying up that which others make a mess of. She likes lifting stains from the carpet, likes to see more light filtering in through the windows. It makes her feel useful, and she's good at it. She likes what her hands make possible, and she likes repeating the same routine, moving from cubicle to cubicle with a calm mind; sometimes she observes how the foam sprouts up from the water's surface, or the very fine trace left behind when the bleach dissolves. She appreciates it if they thank her, though she knows she's invisible to most of them. Who pays attention to the woman's body broadening each year, two arms and two legs and a face, reduced to a uniform? She doesn't need anyone to feel good about what she does, just herself. Occasionally the company calls and asks her to cover for someone and work a double shift, or do a demonstration for a new client. She always says yes, because it's not easy to cover the rent and the rest of the bills all on her own, and still have some left to save. Every month she has less to send Carmen; her mother reproaches her for it, she can't get by on the widow's pension alone, and she suspects that Chico—his hair getting dark, two heads taller than her by now—helps out as much as he can, after his expenses. If that doesn't happen, if she doesn't have to go to some office building in García Noblejas, she sticks to her routine: meets up with Loli and Conchita, or goes to one of Pedro's meetings at the association, and if the mood takes her, joins them for beers afterwards. His friends are now used to her presence, and occasionally, Alfonso will bring his wife along, too. Until that happens, María keeps quiet, and then—with another woman there—slips into the expected role: anecdotes about child-rearing and motherhood, kitchen secrets and beauty tips. Saturday afternoons she saves for herself, and sometimes she goes for a walk in the centre, or stays at home just reading. On Sundays, she eats lunch with Pedro: usually at her place, the two of them, or with María's cousin and her husband;

sometimes at Pedro's, with his mum and his brother, though María finds the atmosphere there depressing, and tends to find ways of getting out of it. After lunch, they have sex, then they watch TV or talk for a while—he usually circles back to conversations from the meetings, so María can have her say, even if only with him—and not long after that, he goes home to make dinner. Neither has ever suggested any variation: María knows that Pedro answers first to his father, who is dead, then to his mother, still alive, and finally, to the brother a few years younger than him, and she also knows that she's unwilling to care for any of them, so they keep their own apartments and try to see each other at least a few times a week. Some of his friends call them "the modern couple." María gets up early every day, except some Sundays. It has been that way for years, ever since the cleaning company hired her, ever since she met Pedro, and she's happy in her apartment with a living room, a bedroom, and a balcony, looking out over a street that will end in another street that will end in another street.

When the phone rings the first time, she'll tell him not to pick up; to stay where he is, naked, lying on his stomach. She has only known two bodies in this way, Pedro's, and Carmen's father's, and she's used to Pedro's by now: if he were ever to crash his motorbike in the square, if they were to ask her to identify the body, María has memorized the location of every freckle, every birthmark. A dark-brown circle in the middle of his right thigh, three freckles on his left hamstring. She looks at them while saying, if it's me they're calling, and even I don't care about picking up, neither should you. Chico knows about Pedro, and Pedro knows about Carmen, Chico, Soledad, her mother, and her older siblings; but María doesn't see why they should know those respective faces or voices, let alone meet in person, so when the phone rings and Pedro gives her that look, it throws her. María can't be sure, but she guesses it's Chico: Sunday nights, she talks with her daughter, some Sunday afternoons her brother calls when he gets home from work, there are times when she doesn't feel like picking up and only answers later on when he calls again. It doesn't bother Chico, nothing can ever puncture his good spirits. Still, María starts to worry when the phone rings again—after just enough time to hang up and dial again—and Pedro jumps out of bed. A few steps and he picks up in the living room.

In bed, after the ringing stops but before Pedro starts talking, María thinks about how happy the weekend has been; maybe today's been just like any other Sunday, but yesterday, certainly. On Saturday, she got home at the same time as always, made a meal for herself, in no hurry—grilled fish, a salad, some fruit—and had a short siesta on the sofa, twenty minutes or so. She took her time getting ready: a bath, a pretty dress—it would have been better to save it for today, so Pedro could have remarked on the colour, the cut of the fabric—the make-up the way she's been doing it for the last few years, darkened eyebrows, red lips. She took the metro to Callao and walked from cinema to cinema along Gran Vía, but none of the films they were showing appealed; she crossed the Plaza de España and walked to Rosales. She had already seen something by that director, maybe at one of the association's screenings, or on a visit to Chico's. She never asked anyone because she knew they wouldn't be interested, and she didn't want them to find out she went alone either—they might feel sorry for her, or worry—so if they asked her about it, she made something up. She didn't find the film all that exciting: faced with the stories other people thought up, she never took long to notice the seams, an inconsistent attitude, a plot that didn't develop the same way it would in real life.

"It's José María, your brother."

José María, she thought while she looked for a nightshirt or a dress to cover up with, as if her brother could sense that she was naked three hundred kilometres away. Her little brother was born on 19th March, and they decided to name him José for that day's saint—although it was also her older brother's name—and the María was for her, his godmother.

"I went to a movie yesterday, Chico. I didn't like it that much. *Fanny and Alexander*, it was called. I had a hard time believing that all those things could happen to one person. Like when you're reading a novel, and the protagonist has the worst luck, so you'll like them more. That's not how life works. Sure, you get your fair share of tragedies, from the time you're born to the time you die. That's the way it goes. Something bad happens to you, and not long after, there's something good to make up for it. I was thinking about it on my way back, on the metro. I went through all that stuff with Carmen, but now I'm OK, I've come to terms with it. That's how it goes, right? And now that I'm talking to you about it, it almost seems like people need that kind of tragedy, because otherwise, they'd have no stories to tell."

"Who did you go with? Did Pedro take you?"

"No, he didn't. I went with my friend's daughter, Laura. The one who's at university."

"How are you doing otherwise, María?"

"Fine, same as ever. No news this week: with work, I've hardly gone out. And it's Sunday, so Pedro's here, and tonight I'll call mum and talk to Carmen. What about you?"

"Fine, fine. This week has been a little strange. Listen, María. I'm going to put someone on who's got something to tell you. We'll talk later."

She keeps all the pictures of her daughter in a box, but the last few months, she's got into the habit of pulling out one that Chico took on a recent trip to the beach. One of their older nephews had offered to drive them to the coast. Carmen, Chico, and her mother got up early and rented a couple of sun loungers at a snack bar in Fuengirola; the four of them took turns sitting in them all day. Chico decided to splurge and reserve a table. They put away the sandwiches Carmen had made and ate fried fish, tomato picadillo by the spoonful, and bread soaked in oil. Her mother agreed to get her feet wet, and the nephew taught Carmen to swim, or at least tried to get her to wade out as far as she safely could. At six o' clock, so they could make it before dark, they went home. Soledad was sorry she hadn't gone, it was days before she got over it.

A few weeks later, María visited on her time off, and Chico told her about it and showed her the pictures he'd taken. Her mother in a loose-fitting floral dress, under the straw umbrella; her nephew showing his broken front tooth, at ease with the imperfection, putting one arm around his grandmother or licking the sardine oil from his fingers. A clumsy photo of Chico, taken by Carmen: her brother is already a man, almost thirty years old, and he crosses his arms over his chest to hide the fat that has been accumulating there; her daughter has cut him off at the knees. Chico is a mystery to María; he spends all his free time at the cinema, or—in the last year, year and a half—taking photos. Their mother scolds him for having the taste of a prince, and he doesn't argue; he spends more than he'd like having film developed or buying movie tickets. Over time, María has learnt to respect his happiness, though she doesn't understand it.

There are more photos of Carmen from that day than of anyone else. Carmen and her cousin on the beach; Carmen drying off with a towel, in the shadow cast by the sun lounger; Carmen making a face at her uncle, maybe because she wants him to stop taking pictures: she holds up her left hand and shows her teeth, mouthing some reproach. In that photo, and the ones that come after—Carmen kneeling in the sand, saying something to her grandmother, or Carmen walking along the shore by herself; María likes the candid ones best—Carmen has become an adult. María gets the sense that the look on her face, that furious wish to remain unobserved, means her daughter has exited childhood, but not yet crossed into adolescence. She flips back several images: even in those last few, Carmen's face seems to have hardened, her hips have widened, and her chest has filled out. In her eyes, which never had much of a spark, were never really childlike, bitterness is stirring.

Ever since someone asked about her daughter in a bar a few years ago—a stranger one night—and she lied about Carmen's age so as not to reveal how young she'd been when she had her, and she didn't describe her, because she knew she had her father's small, dark eyes, but she didn't know the shape of her face, or if she preferred her hair up or down, María has started going to the box of photos from time to time—in the living room, in a drawer where she keeps papers and mementos—to take out the ones Chico gave her. It's part of the last stretch of the day: the ones in which Carmen no longer looks like Carmen, or not the Carmen she thought she knew, but a woman who, before long, will fly the nest. Carmen's hair is still wet because she went all the way under, and it's up in an improvised bun: a ponytail she wraps around itself and secures with a hair tie. She has lowered her bikini straps to avoid tan lines, and although her body is turned towards the camera, she's looking away from it, listening to someone. From the order of the images and the two that came before, she suspects that she's talking to her cousin, who may be standing behind Chico. There are the eyes, tiny, so inexpressive; the father's eyes, which María would recognize—whether or not she wanted to—in any face she came across. There are the thick brows, the very pale skin; you can't see them in the photo, because of the quality of the print, but her memory calls up the blue lines on Carmen's arms. Her nose begins just under her eyebrows, thin at the top and wide at the bottom; virtually funnel-shaped. Her lips are thick; her ears, flush to the sides of her head; her hair is light brown and very thin, María remembers how carefully she would brush it for her.

Her face is square, her forehead wide, her features drawn with a firm hand. She's a little over a metre-sixty, neither fat nor thin, her breasts have matured quite a bit in the last year. María repeats this description out loud every two or three days so she won't forget it. As for what Carmen is like inside, she doesn't really know: a scant five-minute catch-up every Sunday night, and when María visits, she tries hard to plan some activity for the two of them, which Carmen always cancels because her head hurts or she'd rather stay in. It pains her, she tells Chico, that the girl has no sense of humour, but on the other hand, she's very mature for her age. That summer, she stopped going to school because she didn't like studying, and in September she's due to start at one of the department stores in the town. Now, on her way home, Carmen stops by the restaurant where Chico works, killing time over a glass of water, and they walk back together, he to his apartment, and she with him, some nights. María hopes she'll keep her pay cheque for herself, trusting that one day she'll want to go back to school, start her own business, where no one can order her around.

It's a Monday. She's had a hard time closing her eyes tonight, let alone sleeping; Pedro went home to make sure everything was OK, not trusting his mother to tell him otherwise over the phone, and after dinner, he came back to María's to be with her. He lasted until after midnight. He didn't sleep there—he never has; María has never begun a day waking up beside a man—but he did stay quiet next to her, first on the couch, holding her hand, then lying down, trying to get her to rest. A whimper prefaced the weeping: María, who hadn't cried when Irene died, who hadn't cried when her father died, now couldn't stop. Pedro called a few minutes ahead of the alarm clock. I haven't slept, she said when she picked up. I haven't either, he said. How are you doing, María? Not good, but it'll pass; everything always does. I'm leaving for work soon. Me too. I'll call you when I get home. I'll be here. You don't have to come over. I was going to go for coffee with Conchita's daughter today, and give back some of her books. It might be good for me to be around someone who doesn't know. Kisses. Kisses to you too. Although the October sun is still kind, and María is ready so early—the same uniform Monday to Saturday, blue trousers and baggy white shirt, trainers so her feet won't hurt later—that she could afford the red lights, even the one near the station that takes so long to change, in spite of all that, today, she needs an empty mind, routine, something to occupy her mind. She takes the metro, finds it impossible to read, she overhears the conversations of the other early risers: they talk about their weekends, the family meal on Sunday, the problems their children are having at school. She gives up her seat to a pregnant woman and moves to the other side of the car: the dialogues repeat; co-workers, neighbours, people who see each other morning after morning after morning. That living landscape seems strange to her, so different from the one she would have traversed if she had taken the bus: from the functional buildings to the beautiful ones, a handful of monuments, and afterwards, the shift to being surrounded by skyscrapers; like travelling back and forth in time. Some of the faces she recognizes, of course: a woman who lives a few doors down from her, whom she often sees at the butcher's, and a man who looks a lot like one from her first years at the association, maybe it is him, or maybe it's his brother; the features are the same, but he either doesn't recognize her or pretends not to. She has learnt to respect other people's desire for silence. Maybe that's what it is, with the man; whatever it is, it's his business.

She arrives at the building ahead of Teresa: by fifteen or twenty minutes, she thinks when she gets off the metro; when she sees the clocks in the lobby, she discovers it's more than that. She decides to go ahead on her own and, if she finishes early, get a start on some of Teresa's work. She removes the thin layer of dust that has gathered on the filing cabinets in the last two days; she forces water and soap against a coffee ring on a table. She looks at the desks, some with framed family photos, otherwise mostly identical: papers and pens, files and ashtrays, typewriters—one of the companies in the building has electric ones, and she runs a duster over them, careful not to do any damage. She opens some windows, grateful for the cool wind; she breathes in the lemony scent of the floor cleaner, finishes what she didn't have time for the previous Saturday. Her jobs complete, and Teresa still yet to arrive, María takes the cleaning cart and shuts herself up in the storeroom and cries. It isn't very often that she cries, almost never. She didn't cry on leaving Carmen with her parents and moving to Madrid; she never cried when she got fired from a job. It embarrassed her, crying in front of Pedro the previous night, she regretted making herself vulnerable, and when he left she allowed herself to weep, hoping to tire herself out that way and maybe get a little sleep. But she hadn't.

She's pulled herself together by the time Teresa arrives.
Her eyes are red, and she hasn't been able to hide the dark
circles underneath them with make-up. Teresa asks if everything's OK, if something's happened, María offers to go
around the different offices with her, until the employees
arrive and they have to move on to the common areas, so
as not to disturb anyone. Teresa hums, she avoids silence;
she improvises anecdotes, jumping from decade to decade
to keep María's mind off whatever it is. A few weeks ago she
was walking in the city centre and, stepping over a grate,
her skirt flew up in the stream of air, and everyone saw her
underwear, she had to go in for a cup of tea somewhere just
to calm down. María appreciates Teresa's efforts, she forces a
smile so she'll relax. Cleaning hallways and receptions, with
the radios as background noise, both of them now quiet; one
occasionally comments on a headline, the other nods. When
the shift ends, they say goodbye. María goes to return her
cart to the storeroom and feels Teresa's hand on her back.

"I won't ask you to tell me what happened; I don't need
to know. But I'm here for you, whatever you need."

The offer doesn't seem genuine to María. She and Teresa
hardly know each other. What sense would there be in telling her about the phone call, describing what she heard
and what she felt? How could Teresa empathize, knowing
nothing about the rest of the characters in her story? She
doesn't remember ever mentioning Carmen. María would
have to go back to the beginning, when she had just turned
sixteen, and she and Soledad were doing alterations for a
seamstress: from morning to night, thread and needle and
precision, no machines at all. One day Chico woke up with

a very high fever, and their mother was afraid it would get worse if he went out to do his delivery and pickups, so María had to walk to the avenue and catch the bus to the city centre, to make sure his round was done and the day's money not lost. A single street was her entire world: an invisible border lay two or three blocks from her house, attending school had barely meant going beyond it—she had dropped out a few years before—and now, she crossed it only on her mother's arm. But a man sat down next to her on the bus, and his eyes, dark and very small, roused her curiosity. She answered his questions: my name is María, I'm sixteen, yes, I live on this street, at number fifteen, with my parents and two younger siblings, the older ones are married and living on their own. In the days that followed, with Chico still recovering and María filling in for him, the man got into the habit of sitting down next to her, and going on with his questions: I don't mind sewing, and it keeps me busy, but I don't want to do it forever, maybe I'll try something else later on; staying in school never occurred to me, it never seemed possible, we can always use a little extra money at home, and my younger brother, he's the really smart one. Later, after Chico got better, María ran into the man from the bus one morning when she and her siblings went out to the square to sit in the sun. The man asked her over several times, and María didn't say no. The last time she went, it was already cold out. Chico liked to put his hand on her belly, in the final months, and feel the baby kick; when Carmen was born, her father told María that his brother in Madrid had gotten her a job. María didn't say no then either. The first few times she went home, she talked about wanting to save up a little money, rent a place on her own, take Carmen with her. Chico kept her from telling their parents at first; years later, she worked up the courage, but her mother wouldn't allow it. What was she to Carmen? Someone who showed up two or three times a year, on hand in moments neither of sickness nor happiness; missing from all the memories she would return to as an adult. And what was Carmen to her? Her mother took care of her all day long. Who would look after Carmen in Madrid, when María was working? How would she fit a baby, soon enough a little girl, soon enough a teenager, into her routine? María pressed from time to time, at Christmas, when she visited during the summer; she asked how much money—how much more money—she needed for her daughter to come and live with her. She did the maths, she saved and saved. The last time she asked— now with money enough that the two of them could make a start—her mother told her that Carmen would rather stay there, with them. Now, if she told Teresa all of that, would she understand why she was crying? She didn't want to mention the phone call: the story Carmen told her, that she already knows; she had been through it herself when she was a few years older than her daughter. But that's not even what bothers her, because she knows her daughter will bear the consequences the same way she did, will wear a borrowed wedding dress, will keep the photos from that day in a box so no one sees her belly. What bothered her was the tone, the ending; the way she said goodbye. She could say, for example:

"She called me 'María,' Teresa. Not 'mother,' not 'mum': she used my name. She told me not to bother showing up, because it's going to be a big day for her, and there's no reason I should pretend to care now, if I never really have."

But it would be hard for María to suddenly come out with all of that, since they've never gone beyond casual conversation, never opened any space for the sharing of secrets; to tell her would have meant forcing that connection, letting all her feelings come tumbling out about her relationship with Carmen, the wedding, the birth. Would she even hear about any of it? Would Carmen call to tell her? Would Chico? She desperately wants it to be a boy.

María smiles at Teresa, hugs her, and says thank you, thank you so much. She pushes her cleaning cart into the storeroom and hurries out so that she gets away a little ahead of her co-worker, so that she can leave on her own. She'll try not to think on the journey home, but she'll be thinking the whole time: about the conversation with Carmen, about Chico begging her to forgive him for not having suspected, about Pedro's clumsy attempts to console her. On the metro, a woman tells another that her daughter is pregnant, that in five months she'll be a grandmother. Well, I won't, María feels like saying, but she doesn't, afraid they'll think she's crazy: you'll never guess what happened on the metro this afternoon. Keep quiet and act like everything's fine, that's the best way to forget. At home, she eats lunch and waits for Laura to arrive, they chat about this and that. At one point María asks:

"Can you recommend a novel for me? Or short stories? Something with the same themes we've been reading about."

I want the comfort of reading stories worse than my own.

Money's the thing: not having enough is the thing. Every one of the situations that brought María here—"here" being the one-bedroom apartment in Carabanchel, the metro ride to Nuevos Ministerios—would have unfolded differently if there'd been money. She and Soledad and Chico left school because the family needed money; for money, she filled in for her brother one morning when he was sick, so they wouldn't lose that day's earnings. If her parents had had money back then—if they were well enough to earn it, had enough of it to stay well—would she have met that man, on that bus? They walked the same streets, they would have crossed paths at the corner shop, maybe, or one Sunday, at her brother's bar. But with money, without a lack of money, María would have been walking to school then, setting off from a big house with a bedroom of her own. For money, she had to leave home before she was ready, replace her daughter's scent with that of someone else's son. The apartment she lives in is the apartment she can afford, not the apartment she'd like to have, and her job is the one, being who she is, having the money she's had, to which she could aspire. Everything she hasn't experienced has been because of a lack of money. The holidays she hasn't taken, the dresses she's decided not to buy, eating at home with Pedro, to save a little. The money she sent to her mother wasn't enough to make Carmen happy; maybe it seemed like too little, maybe she couldn't appreciate—someday—that she was absent because of just that: money. But because of something else too: because she's a woman. When the man on the bus asked her a question, she chose to answer, because saying nothing seemed rude. She endured the pregnancy at home, hidden away, sewing in the backyard so she could at least see the sky. What was he doing then? He took his life elsewhere: his job, his family, starting over in another neighbourhood. Some nights she's run all the way to the door of her building, when it got dark before it was even late; she has kept quiet in meetings for years, listening to her arguments, her ideas, in Pedro's mouth.

María thinks about things you can buy, things you can buy without anyone raising an eyebrow when a woman pays for them. The metro card she uses to go from home to work, from work to home. A comfortable sofa. The washing machine. The fridge. The food: what she buys, and also, in a way, what she rules out because of the price. The beers she has after meetings, when Pedro or some other friend isn't paying. The discomfort when someone announces that the next round is on him, since that means it'll eventually be her turn. A bouquet of flowers she got herself a few days ago. The plants, too: the water and sun make them grow, but she bought them, the seeds, the little clay pots that she'd like to paint someday, when she has the time and the money. Money can buy all that: money can get you anything. With money, she pays the rent on the apartment she lives in alone, where Pedro sometimes comes to see her; without money, she'd have to live with him, at his parents' place, taking care of his mother and his brother, tied to whatever wages they thought she was worth, tied to the affection she would have to pretend to feel for them. María has been sharing out money since the day she started earning it. She gave her mother every céntimo she made at the sewing shop. Her salary from the first house, too: something for her aunt and uncle, for her cousin's room, and the rest back to her mother, for Carmen, the same dark eyes as the man on the bus; María kept a little for herself, to get around, so she could buy herself something someday. It didn't matter what; anything just to make the possessive itself hers again: *my* skirt, *my* earrings. When she was earning a bit more, she tried to find herself an apartment, a small one, little more than a single bedroom on the same street where she lives now, taking advantage when the people who'd lived there before went back to their villages in Extremadura, in Andalucía: it didn't hurt that her boss said she was reliable and decent, but she rented it with money; money also bespeaks reliability, decency. María kept sending money home, she got a job that wasn't any better but that paid a little more, rented a bigger apartment: a living room, a bedroom, a kitchen, a bathroom. She wanted to buy, little by little, the roof over her head—the roof under which she would die—but she had to save up for a deposit; if she managed, it would take twice as long as it did for everyone else because she was doing it alone. She thinks that has to do with money, too. Is there anything money can't buy? Maybe she should have saved more money for Carmen. Maybe she should have given her more extravagant gifts: not the doll she could afford, but the one all her classmates were playing with. Maybe when María learnt that Carmen had dropped out, she should have offered her something else: university, the two of them living together. Surely Conchita's daughter would have helped them. What would Carmen have wanted to be? What was she good at? María had no idea. How must her daughter feel about money?

BEAUTY

Madrid, 2015

T HE ALARM ON HER PHONE goes off. Alicia wakes up. If beauty was a thing that mattered to her even slightly, then at this moment—at the alarm on her phone going off, and her waking up—she would also hear the other alarms on her floor, on the floor above, two buildings down: strangers who barely interact when taking out the rubbish, all now together in this, all bleary-eyed as the same alarm, from the same make of mobile phone, sounds on their night tables. A song comes in a second or so later, because the clock on one phone isn't synchronized; a second goes off early, ironing out the shock. Alicia has no time to be moved by such nonsense as coincidence; the alarm goes off, she wakes up.

Depending on the shift she's been assigned, Alicia either leaves for work before Nando, or after. She doesn't feel like talking in the morning, so either way, he tries not to bother her; sometimes she watches him walk to the bathroom on tiptoe, trying to make as little noise as possible. If Alicia has a late shift, the morning is given over to cleaning and errands, sometimes a walk through the neighbourhood, maybe a movie. But if she's working the early, she'll have taken the first metro, changed to the blue line at Gran Vía, rushed to the shop so the tourists can buy jellybeans and miniature versions of the Puerta de Alcalá; she'll go back the same way, have a long lunch, clean and do the shopping and walk, et cetera, to kill time until Nando arrives. Alicia doesn't enjoy her work, but it keeps her occupied: it allows her to watch people. If she cared about beauty at all, she would justify it as a kind of curiosity, as if she had an anthropologist peeking out from inside her: the stunning diversity of the human species, different faces, different attitudes, men and women, big and small, rich and poor—no, not the poor: the poor take the bus—all of them the same when they drop their trousers, when they lift their skirts, zippers down, buttons unbuttoned, men and women, big and small, the rich and whoever else can pay their bills and still take the train out on holidays and weekends, all made equal taking a piss at Atocha station. Initially, Alicia thought it was a shame you had to pay to use the station toilets, because from her position behind the counter she had a clear view of the people going in to use the facilities: she liked guessing which of them kept their true desires hidden at home, who was looking for quick sex, if they wanted to charge or pay. When whoever was on the next shift showed up, if it weren't for those required céntimos, she could have delayed her return home, slipped into a stall in the men's bathroom and waited until she heard panting or a plea, one body against another; something to justify pretending to be in a rush to get to the turnstiles, getting on the blue line, transferring to the green line at Gran Vía, rooting around for her keys in her handbag, then tossing it near the door until the next day.

But no: maybe then, in a way, Alicia had cared about beauty a little. Now, the people who use the station bathrooms seem utterly mediocre to her. Every so often, when she's not busy answering some customer's questions, she watches out of habit as people go in and out of the men's. She can easily tell by now which tourists are willing to pay sixty céntimos so that every five minutes someone wipes the droplets from the toilet seat, refills the foam soap dispenser, makes sure no vagrants have slipped in with sixty céntimos they've scraped together, interfering with the minimalist décor. They walk quickly and resolutely, one hand accustomed to holding a suitcase—a small, hard-shell suitcase, barely two changes of clothes for two days—the other holding a phone. Their thumbs tap, and tap, and tap. In their apartments, do their alarms go off at the same time as the ones on the floor above, as the ones in apartments two buildings down? How thick are the walls of their homes? Others stick their heads inside the shop, ask timidly if there's a free toilet; they say it just like that: a free toilet. They don't want to pay, or they can't: they're pulling along huge suitcases, worn-out fabric and spring-loaded clasps, so they can cram in a coat, several jumpers; sometimes they drag oversized chequered shopping bags with them, from some charity shop, and they ask about that, a free toilet. Alicia says there isn't one, over there—she points—they charge sixty céntimos, but it's always clean. If she cared at all about beauty, she would think the kind she cared about was the total opposite anyway: things that were dirty or broken. But she takes her time as she tells them it's always clean, and then she looks at them silently, in case they want to buy a bar of chocolate for the trip.

The alarm on her phone goes off. Alicia wakes up. Moments before, as with every night of her life, she was dreaming of her father hanging himself from a tree.

Then there's the moment when Alicia pretends she's in a hurry, one step after another to the turnstiles, to the blue line, transferring at Gran Vía, catching the green line, rooting around for her keys in her handbag—in her handbag, her keys, her purse, a large menstrual pad in case she comes on early, her phone charger, a packet of tissues, an apple that's going bad—she tosses the handbag near the door until the next day. She gets home around midday, if she works the early shift; she gets home at night if she works the late. She likes that better, the second shift, because she doesn't have to wake up early, and it's less likely that she'll run into anyone she knows; a small portion of the night with Nando, small enough that the football reruns have already finished by the time she gets in. But sometimes she trades it, because a co-worker—always a woman, without fail—asks her to, and Alicia does her the favour so she can drop her son off at nursery or primary or secondary school or university, can wipe his arse and brush the biscuit crumbs off him, and don't worry, his father or his grandmother or his grandfather or his aunt will pick him up in the afternoon, while I'm work-ing. When Alicia gives up her favourite shift, she feels like a superhero, just like when the people in the bathroom that costs sixty céntimos try hard to aim their urine stream so it stays inside the bowl, a little solidarity among the working class: the personal is political.

If Alicia works the early, there's nothing to get her out of an afternoon spent with Nando. Where should we meet, he asks over WhatsApp, as if they haven't been sharing an apartment since three weeks after the second night they slept together—that's how he puts it, "slept together," because he thinks it's discreet, and he doesn't want to offend her. She finds his euphemisms ridiculous, though part of her enjoys his clumsy attempts to hide his ignorance. She still feels strange picking him up at the bus stop, the two of them walking side by side down Alcalá—almost as far as the motorway, a detail Nando omits and Alicia stresses—recognizing the smell of his shit every morning. Soon, they'll celebrate their seventh anniversary. When Alicia gets off in the evening, she waits until eight, when the bus stops on the other side of the square, and they walk the few minutes home together. Sometimes he changes clothes without showering, or else—in the winter especially—he says he can't even be bothered to do that. They have a beer, two, some salty pepitos and raisins, and by then Javito and Isabel are there and order a round, later it'll be Salva and Natalia, then, finally, Edu and Rocío, because they work on the other side of Madrid, for all that they'd rather not leave the neighbourhood. Alicia is fascinated by the way a couple becomes an indivisible element, how her name loses value on its own, and takes on meaning in combination with another: daily life defined by mathematical science. Javito and Isabel, Salva and Natalia, Edu and Rocío, Nando and Alicia: the men come first in the list, always with the diminutive, so you feel right at home— neighbourhood boys, old friends; they're held together by, *wink-wink*, the copulative conjunction; and the women finish off the full name, I-sa-bel, Na-ta-lia, Ro-cí-o, A-li-cia, never Isa or Nati or Roci or Ali, because women deserve respect. The mergers are more than conceptual; they also occur on the physical plane. Alicia doesn't know if Edu and Rocío talked as they do now before they met or if they've contaminated each other, but she's often distracted by the frantic gestures they make to emphasize any comment, and Javito's new highlights are the same shade of blond as Isabel's hair, and Salva and Natalia are getting fat in tandem. Alicia wonders if her nose has curved like Nando's, if she looks like an out-of-place baby, if she's growing a paunch.

They don't stand out. There are several groups like theirs that meet at the bar day after day, interchangeable: three or four couples, two members of the group always united by a friendship that dates back to the playground, another recruited through the art and labour of love. The Latinos meet at bars that serve fried chicken, and the Chinese you never see anywhere. Nando and Alicia live one street back, less than a five-minute walk. The clientele midweek is around thirty-something, almost forty, forty-something; the younger crowd is out in the square or at the pool halls, and the older ones are at the taverns—chairs enough for everyone, paper table mats—where they'll end up soon enough. Salva and Natalia broke the symmetry three years ago, when she got pregnant with Martina, and then Javito and Isabel, a few months after, when little Javier, *Javierín*, was born. At home, where no one can hear them, Nando calls him Javierón—*big* Javier—and wonders how he fits in his carrier, the creases of his thighs and arms piling up. One night, after too many beers, Nando asked if Alicia thought Isabel would take

Javierón to the altar when they got married, in a gigantic baby sling, and first Alicia opened her mouth, astonished, then she let out a loud laugh, and another, and she went on laughing like that for minutes. She was relieved he'd said it at home and not at the bar—she knows it would have bothered Javito and Isabel, and that Nando doesn't like those kinds of situations; Alicia would have had to put up with his whining—but it surprised her that Nando contained an iota of wit, even an iota of cruelty. Maybe that's why, even though it was a Tuesday, they fucked before bed.

Alicia knows that Natalia would rather not have any more kids, because she told her while she was changing Martina—who sleeps in the pram, barely cries, and usually observes them with indifference: she's so easy that Natalia doesn't want to risk having a baby that would make their lives more difficult; on the other hand, she knows that Isabel wants to, but Javito is resisting because several of his co-workers were fired a few months ago and he was given no reassurances that he wouldn't be next. At their get-togethers—so-called—they chat about the co-workers they can make fun of almost without trying, about corruption and La Liga, but no one mentions motherhood. Edu and Rocío have been trying for years but haven't managed it: he refuses to do the fertility tests, he told Nando and Nando told Alicia, and Rocío did them in secret, and they said she needed a treatment to induce ovulation, she told Alicia and Alicia told Nando. Alicia told Nando, adding that the problem wasn't *with* Edu, it *was* Edu. Nando said he would rather not involve himself in other people's business, and that they still had time. He did, Alicia said, but Rocío, not so much, and Nando got up from the sofa to go to the bathroom, and instead of coming back, just got into bed. No one asks about them: no one asks her, at least—they know everything they need to know already: Alicia, thirty years old, father killed himself, doesn't talk to her mother or sister, calls her uncle sometimes just to check he isn't dead—and she imagines that when they ask Nando, he repeats the arguments she's made so many times already. That's funny, she thinks, because really, they aren't even hers: she picks them up on the metro, queueing to check out at Primark, and adapts them to their situation. After all, that's what we do, day after day: we imitate actions, reproduce gestures, adapt them so we can survive.

It worries Nando. Soon, he'll turn forty—he wants to throw a huge party, he keeps saying, a huge party; the idea terrifies Alicia—and he doesn't want to be turning sixty when his kid goes off to university. To Alicia, the thought of giving birth to a child, raising a child, seems ridiculous enough, but it's complete nonsense to think that his son—his son!—would ever be going to university: Fernandito, head of state, winner of a Nobel Prize in Mathematics, cancer cure developer, son of Nando and Alicia, raised in a bar in Canillejas, where he would sleep in a pram that used to belong to Martina. After they'd lived together for two or three years, Nando booked dinner at a grill restaurant and asked Alicia to marry him. She got up and went to the bathroom: she said she'd had too much to eat, all the meat had upset her stomach, and they went home without having dessert. The next morning she asked him if things weren't just fine already, the two of them together day after day; they didn't need papers—a line she'd read in a magazine at the salon—to make their love or their promise real. Alicia thought of the ex-girlfriend Nando had talked about that first night, and the second and every other night until six months into the relationship, when he seemed to accept that she wouldn't be running off. He explained that he also wanted to be sure the apartment would go to her if anything ever happened to him. Alicia thought about it for a few nights—the nightmares became more intense: in one, her father got out of the car completely mutilated, missing an arm, blood flowing from severed flesh—and said yes, but that she wanted something civil, low-key, without her cousins from the village, or her mother-in-law's friends. They signed the papers at the courthouse, Nando's mother paid for lunch at a neighbourhood bar, no more than thirty people. Although Alicia had talked about Nando with him, she chose not to tell Uncle Chico.

Alicia's list of arguments, here goes. Family isn't determined by blood, but by life itself. I'm not sure I want to expose one more innocent to this cruel world. I don't think I'm cut out for raising a child. Your job is stable, more or less, but I've never had one that lasted more than a minute, and with what we make, it'd be hard to provide for another person. Are we really doing so well that we want to risk our stability with someone who will only make problems for us the next twenty or thirty years? Will you be changing his nappies? Will you be giving him his bottle? Are you going to get up when he's screaming at night? Help him with homework and tests? What if your son is arrogant, hypocritical, a liar? If he gets a rise out of tormenting others? The psychopaths who turn up one day with a rifle and mow down the basketball team, cheerleaders, concerned teachers: they have a father and mother, too. Sure, they may be on TV, but they're real. That fucker who chased your brother down the halls in secondary school, Nando, who threatened to slice off his dick and shove it in his ass or his mouth, he also has a father and a mother. Sure, we might give the world the next Albert Einstein or Frida Kahlo—they just mentioned her in a History Channel documentary, it was really inclusive—but there's also the chance we'd pop out a Hitler or a Pol Pot. When Alicia rattled off all her excuses—just like in those tests in secondary school where you learnt the lesson instead of understanding it, reciting all the information as quickly as possible because if you missed one word, you'd get completely lost—she bit her lip between phrases to keep from bursting out laughing. But for Nando, they were enough; for a few months, he relaxed, he didn't bring it up again, he would stroke Alicia's hair and whisper, Come here, Stalin's mother.

That first night, he didn't seem so bad; just polite, earnest, the same as so many others. He endured Alicia's monologue without interrupting—the first person she'd ever told about her nightly dreams—and kept his mouth shut right to the end, when she told him she would stay over only because she couldn't afford a taxi; when she finally did stop talking, she thought she had gone too far. He offered to give her twenty euros, although it would look pretty bad if he slipped her some cash after they'd slept together—bingo: could "sleep together" be his email password?—and she refused it. She turned over, fell asleep. A few hours later, the light woke her, he'd forgotten to close the blinds, and she carefully climbed out of the bed so as not to wake him, dressed without making a sound, closed the door. In the time it took her to walk to the metro, she had already forgotten about the photo of him with his cycling club—Nando had proudly shared it when Alicia asked, almost as soon as he'd closed the apartment door: the bikes in the foreground, the cyclists arranged behind in two lines, according to height, all of them with black and lime-green gear on, helmets and gloves—and the wooden frame with a picture of a very thin woman, her long hair dyed blond and pulled into a high ponytail, small gold hoop earrings. Alicia guessed from the collar that she was wearing a sky-blue athletic jacket, and she had posed at a scenic viewpoint, a big mountain dominating the background. The street cleaners were collecting shards of beer bottles on the pavement from the night before. Alicia learnt that it took an hour and fourteen minutes to get from the door of Nando's place to the door of her own. Back home, she showered, had some warm milk, and got in bed. She didn't think much about it. Two weeks later, she met someone else, and the same thing a month later, et cetera.

Exactly a year after that, her co-worker—that same co-worker—invited her to her birthday party. A few drinks, a few laughs, it didn't sound like a bad idea: her contract was ending in ten days, and they had already let her know they didn't plan on renewing it. Her boss called her into his office to give her the news, and while he made a string of excuses, Alicia worked out how long she could go without a salary: we're in the worst moment of the financial crisis; I've been incapable of saving any money; it's the bosses' decision, my hands are tied; I've got a few months' unemployment, it might as well be nothing; your contract's expiring soon, so it made the most sense; I'm too old to call Uncle Chico and ask him for help. Alicia thought about how she would have to leave her apartment when she couldn't pay the rent. She would have to go back to sharing, tolerating a stranger's judgements in exchange for the right to use the cutlery and the other seat on the sofa, cleaning up after everyone else—she remembers the mountain of dirty plates in the apartment in Aluche, a little plant pushing up from the crockery—locking herself in her bedroom if she wanted some privacy. The waitress from the bingo hall told her about some new flatmates who had tried to rape her the night after she had moved in, before she'd even had time to open the two boxes of belongings she'd brought along, and another flatmate stealing anything she could get her hands on: money, DVDs, open tubs of moisturizer, even an album of childhood photos.

Alicia hadn't been thinking: of course there were going to be a lot of the same faces as at the previous birthday party. She realized that the moment she walked in and saw him there at the bar. She hadn't thought of him in all that time—nor the epiphany moment of light hitting beer-bottle shards at the entrance to the metro—and yet, there were those extremely long legs, those bulging eyes, he was paying for his beer at the bar. She looked for her co-workers, Paola scolded her for being so late, they had calculated that she must live an hour and ten minutes away, they gave Rocío the group gift. While Alicia was thinking of an excuse to leave before he saw her—I've got my period, I'm a mess, I'm having a hard time with all the work stuff—she felt a hand on the back of her neck. Instead of saying hello, he told her how rude she'd been to leave without a goodbye, to which she replied that he'd made such an impression on her she just didn't want to spoil it. She asked what his name was, because she had forgotten. Nando, I'm Nando, he said, and Alicia realized that he was holding two beers, one in each hand. He handed her one, the glass still cold, she thanked him for it, he turned around and let her get back to Paola. The owner of the bar lowered the shutters—Rocío knew him—turned up the music, and let anyone who wanted to smoke; they brought out sharing plates, a heart-shaped cake. The girls danced a little, Alicia didn't hear his voice again, Paola said how much she would miss her, for a moment, she imagined the contract that wasn't being renewed was Paola's, but then again, what shit luck that would be, she has her mother and kids back in Bolivia. When they raised the shutters, Alicia realized she now had to work out how to get home; she went to the bathroom to figure out what to do, maybe a night bus to Cibeles, and change there to get the one home. She left the bar, and there Nando was again: leaning against a car, nervous, playing with the drawstring on his hoodie, pretending to consult his phone, but he looked up as soon as he heard Alicia ask Rocío where the bus stop was.

"Hey. The bus will take forever. You can stay with me, if you want, and be on your way as soon as you get up. I'll sleep on the couch, don't worry."

His pitiful tone and his strategy—breaking off from the group to fabricate a moment of intimacy—seemed completely pathetic to her, but Alicia decided to accept: better this than the hours she'd otherwise spend on buses, the drunks who'd insist on bending her ear, the fearful, solitary walk the rest of the way back to her apartment. He didn't say goodbye to his friends, and a few steps later, he told her this was it, and Alicia recognized the doorway from a year before. As they were going up the stairs, she thought about how she had never fucked the same man on two different nights because if there was a connection—a housemate or a co-worker they both knew—she begged them never to give out her phone number and always disappeared before morning. Suddenly, she wanted to: the tan lines on his muscled calves, the empty Tupperware stacked up in anticipation of a visit to his mother's.

How was she going to do it? What if he spurned her advances? Maybe his proposal had been sincere, and after she ran off the last time, Nando didn't want to do any more than offer her a blanket until the metro opened back up. No one had ever said no to Alicia, and she had never gone upstairs without a kiss in a bar first, or a hand under her clothes. Nando asked if she wanted a drink, a glass of water or a beer, he didn't have anything else. The arrangement of the trinkets on his shelf hadn't changed, but the photo of the blonde girl had been replaced with one of him with an older woman, his mother, Alicia thought, in the same frame. The same nose as Nando, short hair dyed bright red, a beach in the background. Nando brought out two cans, she opened hers and took a swig. Alicia asked what he was doing these days, and he answered that he was working in a warehouse—he didn't say more than that—in a nearby industrial area, a bus ride away; his uncle was in charge of incoming and outgoing inventory there. Whenever the uncle retires, he'll take over from him, and Nando dreamt of a strange hereditary monarchy of invoices. Alicia didn't say anything else about herself: she had shared enough on that night a year before. She turned so she was facing him, he stayed in front of the TV and stared at the dark screen while he answered her questions. She leant in to pay attention, and paid attention at the same time to the way his body tensed up. It wasn't desire, but the opposite: she was noticing his fear. Nando didn't understand why she had left that way, without saying goodbye, it had been nice, the conversation seemed meaningful, and for weeks after, he thought he had hurt her, or said something out of line. Alicia tried not to laugh imagining him at a loss among discs of packing tape at the warehouse, recreating the pep talk he must have gotten from the rest of the cycling team, and she realized that she was annoyed because he was talking too much, in her head, his voice droning on, isolated words: *first, ex-girlfriend, either, none, then,* and when she heard *then,* something shook Alicia, and then, "I want to sleep with you," she said, "I want to sleep with you tonight." Nando got up, took her hand, and led her to the bedroom, sweet prince of duct tape. After that, the usual round: someone undressing someone else, someone biting a neck or a shoulder, someone moans, someone stares at the stuccoed wall, someone concludes, that was nice, oh yes, nice. Alicia closed her eyes and tried to sleep, and she noticed how Nando slid one arm under her, the other across her chest, his body against hers, his mouth next to her ear.

"Alicia, all I ask is that you be gentle with me."

It was the ridiculousness of that line that prompted her not to leave when the sun came up, to even spend the day there. Nando called the guys from the cycling club first, to let them know they shouldn't wait up for him, that he'd been at a birthday the night before, then he sent a message to his mother, to let her know he'd be over the next morning instead, that he wasn't feeling well after the party. They fucked several times and, mostly, they talked: cycling, the warehouse, their friends from secondary school, his father's illness and her father's death, his excitement when they approved him for the mortgage on the apartment, a beautiful trip to the Pyrenees, his disorientation when the girl decided to end it with him. Alicia found it funny that he chose that word, not angry or upset, but disoriented: as if love were a map. He walked her to the metro, and she gave him her phone number—her real phone number—when they said goodbye. Nando sent her a message when he got back to Ventas, saying he missed her already, and he called her that Tuesday. On Saturday, they met up in La Latina, they decided to share a taxi to her place, the first time Alicia had slept in her own bed with a man. It was a mystery to her: if she kept her eyes closed when they were fucking so she didn't have to look at him, if her first reaction to his stories was mockery, why did she spend a whole week wondering what he was doing, responding to his messages the second they landed in her phone? The disdain she felt for him was deliciously and perversely close to affection. The next weekend, at her place, she told him her contract was coming to an end, that she hadn't found anything else and she would have to leave the apartment, in case he knew of anyone who was looking for a flatmate. Absolutely not: Alicia could stay with him until something came up and she was able to afford her own place again. They moved her clothes and some of her furniture to his place, and she started picking him up at the bus stop, walking side by side with him down Alcalá, getting to know the smell of his morning shit. Almost a year later, thanks to a friend of Nando's uncle, she found a job. By then, he had already fallen in love, and she had grown tired of zeroing in on neighbourhoods, clicking on low square footage and high prices on rental websites. A year or a year and a half after that, Alicia can never be sure, she doesn't remember when, he asked her to marry him, and she put up a fight at first, only to eventually accept it: if you want something, you have to give something up in return. She said yes.

By the time Alicia realized it, she had turned into her mother: those gold bracelets—she remembers less and less of her face, and more of her jangling wrists. How is Carmen? Has she gotten used to making chickpea and spinach stew Monday to Friday, grilled meat and veg on Sundays? Has she ever regretted anything?

Marriage didn't tame Alicia: at first, Nando insisted she tell him what happened between her and her mother and sister, and she said nothing, not wanting to lie. Nothing happened. Sometimes she would say that they just didn't get along, and he would get annoyed, because a mother and a sister aren't there for you to get along with, you don't meet up with them for drinks or tell them your secrets. Nando encouraged her to invite Uncle Chico to Madrid, he wanted to meet him, and Alicia responded by calling less and less frequently, once every two weeks, once every month, once every two or three months. She couldn't refuse to engage with his family: she tolerated beach trips with his mother—his brother was off living his life—but she asked Nando to go alone for the first leg. If his mother booked an apartment for a week, they left on Sunday, and Alicia joined them on Wednesday or Thursday. That way, you can enjoy each other's company, Alicia said to her mother-in-law, giving her no possibility of a comeback. For their first trips all together, Nando proposed a deal: one week for the three of them in Oropesa, another week just the two of them. She countered: you two can go ahead in the car, I'll catch the bus midweek, Sunday your mum will go back with your aunt and uncle, and you and I will go somewhere else. Nando agreed.

He left on Sunday, and the Monday Alicia set aside for herself: she turned off her phone, slept in, ate a frozen pizza, took a siesta. Later, she showered, put on the floral dress Isabel gave her—it was too big for her, and just right for Alicia—and walked south for forty or fifty minutes. She spotted the San Blas metro stop and looked for a bar where she could have a drink and a tapa. She sat on the terrace and had one after another; when it got dark, she relocated to the bar, and the waiter caught her eye. Not the kid covering tables outside, curly haired, barely a teenager; the older one, forty-something, with prominent sideburns and eyebrows so thick they were almost one. Alicia couldn't make out his accent because he forced his pronunciation to hide it, as if he were ashamed to erase the "s" from the plural, to reveal an origin that erases the "s" from the plural, in an effort equal to her own. That was the first thing she was attracted to. Then, their conversation, of course: his determination to prove that everyone who was anyone had sat down on the very same bar stool where she was sitting now, the rulers of the world slurping down foam at a dive in San Blas. Alicia knew the steps, she hadn't lost her touch: she listened attentively, stopped drinking and picked at more of the bar snacks—sometimes, when she was out of a job or making very little, she would do that at bars to save money. When the waiter closed up, he asked her if she wanted to have something else in the kitchen, although the rest of the staff had already gone. Alicia went home, and in her nightmare, the dirt smelt like reheated oil. Tuesday morning, she cleaned every room, turned on her phone, and had only one message: Nando, Monday night, he told her that he loved her. She said she loved him too, opened the windows in the living room, and drew back the curtains to air everything out.

It became a part of her routine. In that parenthesis she held for herself when Nando and his mother went on holiday, when they left her alone: some years, Sunday to Wednesday, every night; others, just once, whatever she felt like. She made good use of the time when Nando's uncle was hospitalized and he had to spend a few nights with him; and when he took a day off from the warehouse, or there was a bank holiday and he went on a bike trip with friends from the club. A customer who didn't mind getting home a little later than usual, or a man she noticed in the metro carriage and asked if they didn't know each other from somewhere, if they hadn't met before. She never did it when Nando was waiting at home; not so much to avoid hurting him, more out of convenience.

Now that Alicia is thirty, she'll gradually cease being anyone's lucky day; if she wants to keep the upper hand, she'll have to raise her age limit and lower her standards. She noticed it happening when she turned twenty-five, and also when she gained a little weight: the formerly instantaneous responses now took a little longer to obtain. That's why she went back to her early impulses, the ones she had set aside out of shame: not Miguelín's stutter or Juan Antonio López's psoriasis, but the boy next to her in class whose fingers were webbed, the guy who sometimes ate at the restaurant and whose legs were cut off below the knee. Alicia preferred mediocrity by far: an attraction to physical disabilities seemed just too obvious. It's not that she thinks she's brilliant, especially not with the biography she's had, but she does respect the intelligence that has enabled her to survive. That poor sucker from university, Diego, determined to keep his job a secret, though he always smelt of fish, and to list off the same four or five well-known directors, laying them out as if he alone could access the complex secrets of their art. Nando himself, the ridiculous excitement with which he leapt onto his bike every Sunday morning, in the midst of a pack of equally dull men. Alicia liked that sort of thing: a not very interesting person pretending to be someone who was, to the point of caricature. That was it. But with time, those ridiculous men have become less interested in her, her wrinkled hands, the big mole becoming more noticeable on her face, the bags under her eyes; they also have wrinkles and moles and bags under their eyes, and if they give in to a woman like them, they'd rather it be someone gentle, someone who will take in their performance without scorn. Alicia knows they aren't easy to find, and since she has no time to waste, she'd rather make safe bets: men around the age her father would be now, men her age or a little older with an obvious disability, like the ones she would at once notice and reject as a teenager. A severe limp, a speech impediment. Sick people don't interest her—not yet.

There are times when Alicia thinks she sees some of her features, or Eva's, or her mother's, or Uncle Chico's, in a woman sitting across from her on the metro, in the grandmother who presents her grandchild with a lollipop at the station. Uncle Chico's last names are so common that if Alicia did want to look for her mother's mother, she would get dozens of results. What if she were disappointed? What if genes determine your character, not just your eye colour or the shape of your mouth? Alicia used to wonder about her, when she first moved to Madrid, imagining what might happen if they crossed paths; very soon, she had more important things to think about, and she stopped wondering. All her life, she's been asking herself: why do we do what we do? Maybe I should have studied philosophy, she hears the man say the moment she thinks it, she can't tell if he's giving advice or criticism. Why did I go up those stairs and ask him to sleep with me; where would I go if this ended; this would have ended already if I had anywhere to go; if I had anywhere to go, it would never have started. All her life, she's been asking herself: Why did my father kill himself? Because of money? Did my father feel incapable of shouldering his debts, of taking on the payments and moving forward? Her mother had done it with relative ease: she swallowed her pride and started over. Or did her father do it because he was too scared to tell her mother that the life he'd promised had foundations so weak it would crumble before she had even set foot inside it? What percentage of the blame belonged to him, the body of the limping man? What percentage belonged to her mother? What about Eva, and her? Eva, who innocently took those poor girls on a tour of her house of a thousand TVs, what pleasure Alicia sensed in the two of them when they understood the meaning of her mother's words, what happy lives she imagined them living, happy in the thought of Alicia's downfall, and Eva's, and Carmen's. When she was little, Alicia would go to the exact centre of the living room so she could contemplate the outside world without being seen: she wanted to understand what was going on so she could avoid being struck by some tragedy she hadn't seen coming. And yet at the same time she didn't want to be involved in any of it—the children's games, her classmates walking together, adults on their way home from work. She wanted her life in its entirety to unfold in that minuscule space, just big enough for the feet of a girl eleven, twelve, thirteen years old; without needing to eat or sleep, or talk to anyone, just observing reality, not plunging into it. But her mother shattered that wish, her hands soft from avoiding work, the ambition to have more than her share, to hide—shopping bags from El Corte Inglés, make-up purchased on weekend trips to Madrid and Barcelona—the place she came from, the bedroom she'd shared with Uncle Chico and Aunt Soledad, the habits of someone who's had nothing and suddenly doesn't have everything, but almost: a pair of shoes you try out for the first time on the day you're faced with a long walk, shoes whose beauty blinds you but doesn't mask the pain they impart with each step. That precise spot in the living room, at the edge of her adolescence: that's where Alicia wants to be, in the time when there were still nights without nightmares, when her dreams were still full of kisses from handsome boys and big houses she might still get to live in.

JOY

Madrid, 1998

H E ALWAYS TAKES THE AISLE SEAT: on buses, on trains, on planes, stands there in silence while María settles in next to the window, and then follows suit and flops down. It makes him anxious when he's not the one in charge of the vehicle, so if he's not driving—even if they're going only a few streets in the neighbourhood—he refuses to talk on the journey, as if any unanticipated sound might alert him to an oversight: the snoring of someone asleep at the wheel, the screech of a truck trailer decoupling from the cab. If María asks a question or comments on the weather, do you want a bite of this sandwich, I don't think we're going to get there on time, he begs quiet, index finger to his lips, even shushes her, as though the sound might drown out the imminent accident. So if they're travelling outside the city, María always brings a puzzle book in her bag. Over the years, she has learnt to keep quiet in those situations, but there are others in which she has gotten used to speaking up. His friends joke that it's her wearing the trousers; it would be funny if not for the fact that every morning, before pouring his coffee, he checks the way his fit in the mirror. At this point, metaphors aren't really doing it for María: she would rather say what happened, exactly as it happened.

This afternoon, they're on their way back from the movies: they took advantage of the midweek two-for-one tickets, walked twenty minutes to the bus terminal, got on the bus home straight afterwards. Pedro travels in silence, the other passengers' conversations putting him on edge; they distract him from monitoring the driver's potential mistakes. When he brakes at an amber light, he strikes his thigh with his fist, and when he makes an abrupt stop—a girl forgot to push the button to request it—he blurts out a "Come on!" and María is taken aback. She's not sure if she wants him to offer to stay on past his stop, walk her home, share a quick meal, go to bed. She likes things as they are: at first, they lived apart because he didn't want to involve her in caring for his family—three of them sick—when he hardly knew her, and later on, because the idea of taking care of someone with whom she had no real connection made her uncomfortable. When she changed Pedro's mother's nappy, would she remember changing her daughter's in those first weeks of her life? What would happen if she forgot to give Pedro's brother his pills? Would she be the cause of a crisis? Would he turn his violence towards her? What we don't see doesn't exist: Pedro feeding his father, carrying his mother in his arms, or dodging a blow from his brother. He would tell her about it as casually as someone describing an uneventful day, I woke up, I worked for eight hours, I ate an omelette, my brother threatened me with a knife, because for the last few weeks, he's been hiding his pill on one side of his mouth and spitting it out without me realizing, while my mother complained about how it felt to have pissed herself, while my father wiped a strand of drool from his mouth. At first, she would visit them some Sundays, but she ended up asking if they could meet up just the two of them. A long enough walk forced the distance: father, mother, brother, figures she could recognize, thanks to some photos; she knew they existed, but in his stories, she saw them almost as stock fictional characters, sick father, sick mother, sick brother.

Carmen tiptoes through conversations with Chico, a body that never takes shape: Pedro never brings her up, either, and it puts him on edge just hearing the name in conversation among strangers, or shouted on the street. After the wedding, Chico tried to force one or two phone calls a year, coinciding with Carmen's visits; he would tell María when to call to catch her: Carmen would report that she was still married, list off children and pregnancies and her husband's achievements, which were, by extension, her own. Just two or three minutes, her voice deeper each time, less familiar, until she vanished, one call, none, silence. From time to time, Chico slipped some detail into the conversation: he worried about Carmen not having a job, being entirely dependent on her husband, he told her that everyone said Eva was just like him, but that he had a certain weakness for Alicia, the older one. Not a weakness, he specified once: a curiosity. Curiosity about the adult she's turning into. No, it's not too soon. Sometimes it feels like she's retracing months like steps, and suddenly, I'm talking to a little girl who stammers, who still has so much to learn, but she's really just putting that on to get a running start: the very next sentence, she's your equal. She's barely thirteen, but has a mind thirty or forty years older, and the demeanour to match, but even so, she *chooses* the diction that sounds natural for someone her age, calling attention just enough. She doesn't mind solitude. She pushes anyone away who tries to get close to her. She looks down on her sister. I don't know why she behaves that way, the father works all day to provide for them, they have everything they could possibly want, and that's why I wonder where that attitude came from, and where it's going to end up.

"How long have we been together, María?"

The question takes María by surprise, and she understands that he means something else by it. Pedro knows better than she does: they celebrate every anniversary, he never forgets her birthday, and he can recite the date of any trip they've made to the coast. Twenty-some years, she thinks to herself, surprised he has set aside his usual attitude on this journey, by choosing to speak.

"A long time. Right?"

"Twenty-four years."

In Pedro's silence, there's space for María to imagine: he asks, and she does the maths; he specifies, the sound coming from his mouth—and the sound it prompts from María's—distracts the driver, and it confirms his superstition. The driver doesn't realize—it's night-time—maybe someone crosses before looking both ways, the impact of a body slamming against the partition of the bus, black blood running towards the gutter; or maybe someone's hurrying home or away from home—a poorly lit stretch of road—he steps on the brakes to avoid the accident, but a woman inside isn't strong enough to hold on and stay upright, the impact of a body slamming against the floor of the bus, their steps tinted

red with blood. That's how María fills the silence Pedro uses
to tell her: hey, it's your turn, you have to say something now.
Then he resumes the speech he practised at home.

"We've been together a long time now. We aren't teenagers, María. What we're doing doesn't make sense."

The glare from the streetlights bounces off the bodies
of passing cars, and from time to time, a flash illuminates a
rubbish bin, or someone walking a dog; outside, there's nothing but darkness, and yet María looks out intently, searching
for something, she doesn't know what: she's avoiding Pedro
and whatever Pedro is telling her. Every few days, he slips
it in:. Sunday, having lunch at the bar, he brought up the
food the two of them could make at home; maybe again on
Thursday or Friday, when they say goodbye to Víctor and his
wife, and they go home together, and Pedro and María hug
and go to their separate apartments. First, Pedro's mother
died—the father having passed long before—and his brother
followed in January, defeated by all the medication. The
nights just after he died, María told Pedro he shouldn't go
home right away, and he moved in temporarily: a suitcase
full of socks, shirts, and underwear, a few pairs of trousers,
the strange feeling of going to bed together and waking up
together day after day. A few days in, María was already
avoiding the conversations before bed, and getting up earlier
than she had to on purpose. Pedro took the hint, put his
dirty clothes in a plastic bag, and went back home. Some
weekends he would force cohabitation and ask María: Now
that he was free of responsibilities, why not live together,
the two of them?

On María's birthday cake, they had written, "Happy Birthday, Mum!" The lettering was in chocolate on the top of a dense meringue, the first layer dry when the slices were cut. The phrase sounded strange to her, not having heard it in such a long time; it might have hurt another woman in her situation, but she understood that almost no one knew her story, and that she should let the mistake slide—there was no malice in it, only ignorance. The younger girls at the association called María that because of all she did taking care of them: if she made too much stew on Sunday, she froze the leftovers because she knew that a lot of them had no time to cook, and when Elvira lost her job and had to give up her apartment, she let her stay at hers. María had struggled to adjust, and she promised herself she would never again offer up her sofa, no matter how much a friend needed it: her solidarity had to end somewhere. Even so, sometimes a woman comes up to her after a meeting and tells her about a friend or about herself, and asks her. And María never says no.

After all these years, María feels she has arrived in the place that belongs to her: on an equal footing with Pedro. Not alongside him, as much as she would have liked that, but certainly in another, similar space. Little by little, she became comfortable raising her hand at meetings, not sitting down with the other women when they went out for drinks afterwards: she wanted to give her opinion on the request made to the city council for a new park, to be part of the decision about the disbursement of the neighbourhood solidarity fund. They all looked at her with astonishment, as if she'd flown in from another planet, even Pedro. I'm your ally, María was trying to tell them; I'm a thinking person like all of you are, I have as much to say as you do, I'm not here just as a yes-woman. Though she knew that wasn't the whole truth: actually she was a better reader, better at reflecting on what she read, she was more eloquent, she could do the job better than they could. Pedro didn't mind any of this, he swore it, but when she showed him up in front of his friends, when she interrupted him, when, more and more frequently, she said in her own words what Pedro had said before in his, then it did make him uncomfortable: he told her so one Sunday in bed—him with the sheet pulled up to his chest, her naked on top of it—"my friends," he stressed, to give María a sense of the gulf between them. María answered back. Where were all the women at the association meetings? Some come along to the bar to socialize, she said; some don't even show up there. But I'm not like them, Pedro. Well, OK, María, if you say so. He closed his eyes, pretended to fall asleep, and the conversation was over.

When she and Laura got organized, they convinced the association to let them use the space for a few hours each afternoon and gathered enough women to get things under-way. It was hard for María to get used to new habits: saying no when the company offered her extra hours—at first, she refused them all and had to work out a new budget; then she got some other women to sign up for shifts, and let herself take one only from time to time—not even sitting down to eat lunch, leftovers from some other meal, hurrying to the space so Laura could head home. Now María gets up too early, it's harder and harder for her to open her eyes, stretch, drag herself to the bathroom; it's a long metro ride to the university, and the trains are old, and the line is slow, and it breaks down constantly, or you have to change trains. Her company contracted her out to the journalism school several months ago, and she's amused to have swapped executives for students. They toss their papers on the floor, she picks up more cigarette butts, but to María it's such a different terrain to move through that she almost enjoys herself; not immensely, of course, but yes, it doesn't bother her as much as it ought to. María doesn't look at their faces much, face after face after face, because at a certain age, all the boys and all the girls look alike to her: but she hears the conversations, their comments on the news, their enthusiasm for movies—often the same ones she watches, she's sure they'd never guess—and that at least provides a little entertainment. For the moment.

María has just turned forty-eight. Forty-eight, she thinks: she tells Laura she's closer to death than to life, and Laura laughs at the melodrama, so unusual for her. On María's birthday cake, they wrote "Happy Birthday, Mum!" and Laura frowned when she saw it and tried to meet María's eyes to communicate that it wasn't her idea, that the girls had been in charge of it. Laura works in the evening and during the day helps the women in the group with their legal questions; advising a woman who wants to separate from her husband but doesn't have any money, helping a girl who has worked nearby for years with her residency application, although she hasn't officially joined yet. Laura left the neighbourhood when she finished her degree and came back four or five years ago, when the financial crisis hit, to live with her mother. She says the same thing again and again, whether it's herself she's talking about or one of the cases from the association: it's a question of money, it's always a question of money. If we had it, not a lot of it, just enough, our lives would be so much simpler. Happier? María sometimes asks. Going into a shop and buying whatever you want, whatever you've decided on, without doing the sums or torturing yourself over it. Laura would turn to her, smiling: María, doesn't that seem like enough happiness to you?

How to explain to Pedro that no, this isn't the right time, there—here—on the bus isn't the right time? OK, he'll say, then when?, and in such a way that it sounds like a threat. Come to my place tonight, María says, emphasizing the possessive—my place, the apartment where I pay the rent, with the money I earn: that's what the possessive means—and we'll talk about it. Here, it feels like you're ambushing me, Pedro. If Pedro raises his voice, if the words he uses hurt her, María won't be able to get off the bus: not in that neighbourhood. One streetlight blinks on and off and the other, on the next block, never turns on; it's a narrow street with many dark doorways, and she doesn't want to risk it. You hear stories about those streets: a woman at the association said a friend's daughter was forced into one of the doorways, another said that near number twenty, a man with a knife comes out when he hears the sound of high heels. Pedro, you know I'm not going to get off here alone, not this late. That's why I want to say all this now, María, he'll tell her: you have nowhere to go, you'll have to hear me out.

What I want to say, the time has come: Pedro has worked it all out, the words, the numbers, the anecdotes he'll use to make his case. I'm not talking about getting married, María, that'd be ridiculous: when we first met, sure, I would have been excited about that, because that's what we were all aiming for, wasn't it? No matter how modern we thought we were back then. But I had my situation, you had yours, maybe that's why we found each other, why we got this far together. Now we've reached a certain age, a white dress and a reception, at this point in our lives? Would the guys take me out for a stag night? It'd mean we pay less tax, so I'm told, but I'm talking about being practical: it's absurd that tonight, after twenty-four years, I don't know if we'll be sleeping in the same bed. Do I really need to pack a suitcase to spend the weekend at your place, after all this time? Fine, no wedding. Fine, we don't live together. But what's so bad about seeing my trousers in your chest of drawers? Not even a toothbrush, María, not even a toothbrush. I have to bring it to your house in my jacket, or wait until I get back, or use yours.

María retains the details of Pedro's speech. The trousers in her chest, her toothbrush against his teeth. Him, what to call him: boyfriend, partner, mate. "Boyfriend" sounds adolescent, it was wrong even when they first met; "partner" suggests a closeness, a cohabitation, that he tries to force and she resists. María resorts to "mate," and when she mentions him, someone usually laughs: "What kind of mate? Your flatmate? Your classmate?" My life-mate, she clarifies: she tries to avoid emotion whenever she can. A white dress, even if they had lent it to her, just like they had done for Carmen: a white wedding dress, for her, with her wrinkles and streaks of grey—she thinks about dying her hair some impossible colour, orange or lime green—a full dress with lace trim; her, at her age, dressed up like a meringue cake, the top layer brittle just like on the one from her birthday. The stag do, what would they get up to, at what bar, Pedro's hard hands on a young girl's firm skin for a moment. At this point in the story, María finds the possibility more comforting than upsetting.

Pedro insists: María, think about it in terms of money. The thing that matters, that always has: money. The return trip from the city centre seems longer today, as if the bus had crossed from one side of the river to the other, and back from that side of the river, though María occasionally recognizes a sign, some shop window, and in that way, calculates how long it will take to get to Pedro's apartment, and then her apartment. What Pedro's trying to say is that if they were living together, she could save the rent and stop wasting her pay cheque. He says he understands that it's an old apartment, and that there are bodies attached to it—two dead in the master bedroom, the father and the mother, both in their sleep, and one on the sofa, in front of the TV; when Pedro got home from work, his brother's body was still warm, the audience applauding on the Channel 3 programme—but maybe they could redecorate it, and he could stay at her place in the interim. Everything Pedro is saying he has written out on the backs of the flyers they slip into the mailbox: on one side, an electrician's ad—Yeison, the phone number, "very economical" underlined—and on the other, the most sentimental aspects of his argument; on one side, a seer from Africa who offers charms and evil eyes, and on the other, his financial rationale. Pedro knows María well, and he knows she'll accept his proposal if he can convince her that living together is the only way to put some money aside. María, look at your hands, Pedro wants to say: look at the cracked skin of your hands, I've never seen your hands any other way, with time, they've been covered in everyone else's shit, one layer and another and another, from this family and that family, this executive and those brats. María, feel your back, Pedro wants to say: isn't it tired of wringing out the mop, of crouching to scrub another difficult stain. María won't always be able to tolerate the pains she keeps quiet about now, and the company has been firing long-standing employees because the Peruvians charge less and work longer hours; the lower salaries offset the severance pay. When you ask for sick leave, who's to say they won't hire someone cheaper to fill your post? There's always someone who needs the money more than you.

OK, Pedro. We redecorate your apartment, your parents' apartment, put a shower in instead of the bath, get rid of the gas stove; we live together. What then? Will I have a place for myself? The entire house will be yours, María: the master bedroom, the smaller one, the kitchen. No, I'm talking about my position within the relationship. Will I have to tell you where I'm going, who I'm going with, if I'll be coming home late? Will you want explanations if I have dinner with Conchita and Laura and we sit around talking afterwards, and it gets late and I end up staying over? Will I have to call so you don't get upset the next day? The only possibility for me when I came into this world was to get married and have kids, to cook and clean the house, and maybe to work outside the home when I wasn't working in it; but I've had a different kind of life, and I don't want to let go of it.

Of course, those aren't the words she says out loud. She thinks them while Pedro weaves his defence, jumping from one argument to the next: a single phone bill, a single electricity bill and water bill, one metro stop less on the way to work, plus the saving on food if we're cooking for two. María, just like you cook for yourself most Sundays, now you'd be cooking for both of us. And with each word Pedro grows a little shorter, his hair thins, the circles under his eyes darken: María sees him as vulnerable, very fragile, just like when he used to ask her to keep quiet at meetings, to sit with the other women when they went out for beers, to let him speak, to let him speak. María stepped aside, and, with Laura's help, formed the women's group at the association, and many nights, she walks right by when she sees them at the bar; she understands that Pedro needs his friends to see him another way, not as the one whose woman—girlfriend, partner, mate—ignored him, became his enemy, rejected a life with him, but as the one who took back the situation, who got her under control. It's not about money, María thinks to herself; it's about power. About showing his friends—who María confused with her own—the power he has over her. Spend less, put some money away, he insists, I'm thinking about you here, it's for your own good; he emphasizes that life—his life—will be unchanged, he'll be perfectly happy if the situation stays the same, with or without her moving in, but *hers* will improve, fewer expenses, your hands and your back, you're forty-eight years old. And you're fifty-four, Pedro; you're missing a few teeth, and you've grown your hair to cover the spots where it's thinning. She doesn't say that because they're referring to different bodies, because he's going on about her health, but she'd be attacking his dignity, and her intention isn't to hurt him: Pedro doesn't deserve the pain, but he doesn't deserve a victory either.

"Pedro, it's a big decision. I'd like some time to think it over. I can't give you an answer here, on the bus."

If María were to agree to Pedro's proposal, what would she be left with? María calls the apartment she rents, the second one since she left her aunt's house, "my place"—in this case, the possessive is a lie—and she would be losing a favourable price and a landlord who's always quick to see to any problems. She never considered buying a place because she could never have saved enough for a deposit, because no bank would approve a mortgage for someone in her situation, so she accepts that trap her own words set for her, "my place," "my apartment," several rooms in the name of a woman who moved back to the village and who prays that María will win the lottery or meet a good man and leave, so she can raise the rent. If she were to agree to live with him, she would have to get rid of her furniture, or some of it; she wouldn't know how to keep her books safe from Pedro's. What couple doesn't force their libraries to cohabit? María needs to preserve the margin notes, the dog-eared pages, the bus or cinema or theatre tickets among them, so when she revisits them years later, the books themselves will tell her when she read them. What if she demanded the smaller bedroom for herself? Chico will visit once a year, if she's lucky; she doesn't need a bed for him. Maybe she could put a nice armchair there, so she could read in it instead of on the sofa or in bed. What will she be left with if she loses her home, which belongs to someone else, her apartment, which belongs to someone else? And if living together doesn't work, and a long, peaceful relationship implodes the moment it becomes normalized? Normal, she's surprised to think in such terms—María doesn't find anything about herself strange, no matter how many people say otherwise: they've been together for a long time and they're still living apart, haven't they considered the alternative? What if she gets annoyed when he leaves the toilet seat up or fails to put the cap back on the shower gel? Again, just like in the movies. Will she have to start again, look for another apartment, buy new furniture, learn another route to the metro stop? Will it be worth it to go from her new place back to her part of the neighbourhood to buy from the same butcher, the same greengrocer? Does she really have to change it all now? It's a question of money, María thinks, and a question of power. That idea rattles around inside her head, while outside her head, on the bus, Pedro keeps on about their living together, the money they'll save, María's ageing body, and she's exhausted, and she's worn out. On the street, where María's looking, other things happen: as the bus approaches its destination, the street broadens into an avenue, and it grows brighter—several streetlights every few metres of pavement—and some of the bars have already set up their summer terraces. I'll have a drink, María thinks, interrupting herself: if Pedro hadn't decided to make this scene now, I would have suggested we go for a drink right over there, ask for some olives, walk back home holding hands. There's another level to what's happening: the people who get on the bus overhear part of Pedro's and María's conversation, and get off wondering who they are. They enjoy thinking up explanations: depending on the ellipsis—if they got on before crossing the Manzanares, after turning onto General Ricardos—that boy who shut off his Discman to listen will say he's a divorcee, and now his lover refuses to make the relationship official, and that woman keeping one eye on her son's tantrum, which has drowned out part of Pedro's monologue, won't understand why María refuses to save her share of the rent. Money, power: it rattles around in her head. At first, she'd thought Pedro was speaking of love and affection, of company, of caring for her in the way he had only cared for his family before. Was she his family now? Who was María's family?

Two names come to mind right away: Chico and Pedro, of course. She hardly speaks to her older brothers, a call on birthdays, another at Christmas, and something broke between her and Soledad when everything broke between her and Carmen: as if she felt guilty for not having been able to keep what happened to María from happening to her; as if she felt Carmen were her responsibility, and she failed. They call each other, they tell each other things, Soledad has visited, but her sister always talks to her as if she's asking for forgiveness. Two more names: Laura, Conchita. The women at the association who are closest to her in age: Maribel, who knows about Carmen, and Mercedes. Some of the younger girls, who call her Mum and listen when she recommends books and movies; even Elisa, who confessed a few weeks in, ashamed, that she thought she'd been lying or playing a joke on them because she never imagined a domestic worker could get something out of those stories. Without really intending to—they would show up at a lunch, at a meeting, queueing to pay at the shoe shop—they've woven María a web of support for when she's sick, when she needs a second opinion.

It's not a question of family, or of love: it's about money. Pedro makes more than she does, though not by much—that hesitation before they order another beer is something they share—and he wouldn't have been able to afford his apartment on his own either. He inherited it because his parents moved into the neighbourhood when nobody else wanted to, and it was cheap, and they both worked. Pedro's brother died, and Pedro outlasted everyone—buyers, landlords, beneficial owners—so that apartment facing the alleyway, too small for four but enough for one or two, went to him. A stroke of luck, a coincidence that affords him a certain advantage—a certain privilege—with respect to María. What arguments can María call on to negotiate? Is her generosity an argument? What about her body? How can she tell Pedro that the way he's offering to care for her isn't the way she wants to be cared for?

"What are you trying to get out of this, Pedro?"

"I don't get it. You think I've got some ulterior motive? I'm doing this for you. I've thought through all of this for you."

"I have a feeling you do. Is there something you're trying to prove? Is this really all about me?"

"María, you can't go on acting like a teenager. You've been living without thinking about the consequences. Maybe sometimes you only drag yourself down, but sometimes, there are other people involved. When you were sixteen or seventeen, sure, you had an excuse, no matter what happened, but you can't keep living your life like you're on your own. Now you're with me: you've been with me for years and years. Will you cross me out, too, the way you've crossed out everyone else? We're not notes you made in one of your notebooks: one line won't stop us existing. We're here. Your daughter, your granddaughters. Your brothers. Me."

"Pedro, let me out. I'm getting off. I'd rather go home alone."

"This isn't your stop, María. It's not even my stop."

María stands and waits for Pedro to get up, or at least to shift his legs so she can move around him. Each defies the other as the bus moves along; she stretches her body to push the stop button. Finally, Pedro gives in, giving her just a handspan of space to squeeze past him.

"We'll talk tomorrow, Pedro. Better tomorrow, once we've calmed down."

Pedro says nothing. María recognizes this part of the neighbourhood, buildings a little taller than hers, with dirty facades: they're once again crossing a stretch of poorly lit roads, but the main drag isn't far off, so she'll be able to get home without having to quicken her step or constantly glance behind her to make sure no one is following. When the bus stops, she doesn't notice the distance between the steps and the pavement, and her right foot collides with the kerb. María falls—flesh, bones, hair streaked grey, wrinkles—and does her best to get up, a woman who ran from the back of the bus to help her calms her down. A few steps later, she raises her hand to her chin and feels the blood breaking through. While she dabs it with a tissue, the bus pulls away, and she watches Pedro passing, back turned.

———

Do they look like me? María is sometimes overwhelmed by the impulse to ask her brother: do any of them look like me? When she thinks about Carmen's daughters—how can she say "granddaughters" when she's no longer part of the family that threw her out?—it's enough for María to look in the mirror: she assigns them light-blue eyes, a chin that dominates the face, thick hair, almost blond in the summer, skin so light that the blood's exact path shows through. When they give Eva her vaccines, do the nurses remark on how easy it is to locate the veins in her arm? On trips to the beach, does Alicia take refuge under the umbrella to avoid getting burnt? Do the two of them play in the sun, the rays collapsing against their tender young skin? Chico told her that one of them, the older one, runs from any sort of contact, while the little one will happily hold a stranger's hand; hearing about those traits brings Eva closer, but she would need to know Alicia to really understand these snippets Chico shares. Sometimes, when he visits, her brother offers to show her a few photos of the girls, or he tells her on the phone that he wants to send a picture from one's communion, from the other's end-of-year party at school, and María asks him not to. She'd rather not know what they look like: that moment spent in front of the mirror imagining is enough for her, her eyes in Eva's face, her hair on Alicia's head. If I don't see them, they don't exist; if one day one of them wants to hear my side of the story, I'd love to tell her, but at the same time I'm not going to go bothering them.

María opens the door to her building; she's feeling so frayed, she almost can't get the key in the lock. She hears a phone ringing as she takes the stairs, thinks maybe it's in her apartment, Pedro calling to apologize, doubtless, thinks to herself she won't pick up. Once she's through the door, yes: the phone ringing is hers. She doesn't answer straight away, and it goes on until it's done the full number of rings and stops; then, barely thirty seconds later, the ringing starts again. María hears it from the bathroom, she disinfects her cut—now she has to go back down to the door onto the street, retrace her steps to make sure she hasn't left a trail of blood—and thinks maybe tomorrow she'll go to the clinic so they can take care of it, avoid any infection. Whoever it is keeps on trying, calling again after the second set of rings. María groans and throws down the towel. She goes through to the living room, doesn't rush, picks up: her brother's voice.

"Thank God, María. Listen, I've been calling all evening. Christ, got you eventually. I shouldn't, but there's something I have to tell you. Something terrible's happened."

NIGHT

Madrid, 2018

THE STATION IS CROWDED. Alicia has to battle through the turnstiles, not because the trains into the centre are full, but because so many people are getting off at Atocha; she almost doesn't make it into a carriage. She mentally swears at her co-worker, who asked if she would cover for her for a little while—it started out as an hour, then turned into two or three—because the friend who watches her kids had left her in the lurch, forcing Alicia to leave work later than planned. She had heard about the protest, had seen the women on Cuesta de Moyano that morning, but she never thought it would affect her: she just wants to get home, grab something from the supermarket for dinner, for no one to bother her. All of the women at the other shops had shown up for work, a woman came up to the counter to hand her a flyer—OUR VOICE IS THE FUTURE!—that Alicia crumpled up and threw in the bin. She passes some very young girls wearing make-up and purple shirts, carrying placards, some of them holding hands, some boys with them; they jostle by as Alicia tries to find a space on the platform. Several of them give her looks for walking the other direction, not towards the exit, but to the blue line to Gran Vía, followed by the green line to Canillejas, followed by the sofa at home. She's not especially curious about what's happening up above, but then a moment comes when she does turn around, deciding to go back, to join them, leave the metro and walk towards Atocha. Something carries her there. From the entrance to the station, she can make out more posters, purple balloons, a loudspeaker chant. Two girls pass by, one of them holding the other's arm: I'm kind of excited, she confides to her friend. Her laughter, suppressed, comes out as a snort.

She goes on without really knowing where to. Logic tells her to go back to Menéndez Palayo or Palos de la Frontera, transfer to the green line at some point, or even take the Acacias or Puerta de Toledo train so she doesn't have to change; she doesn't feel much like walking, but it doesn't bother her either. She's gotten as far as the square: more people streaming in from either side, people who can't move because the leader of the protest isn't moving yet, or because the crowd is far more numerous than they bargained for. Alicia has never felt comfortable in groups of more than five or six; she finds parties overwhelming, and when a friend of a friend joins them at the bar, she'll fake a headache and go home. People to the left, people to the right; clenched fists on all sides. Does Alicia remember when she became dizzy and fell? She can't describe it: her own body hitting the ground. The fall is softened by a body, another body, she collides with one after another and, finally, collapses on the road. She hasn't passed out, hasn't even closed her eyes: heads, shirts, trousers, shoes, then the dirty grey of the roadside, then an emptiness all around her. Several women hold out their hands, but one—the oldest—doesn't wait for her to take one of them, but just grabs Alicia under the arms and tries to haul her up. Since she doesn't quite manage it, stupid old lady, the teenager who's with her—she guesses it's her granddaughter, though Alicia sees no trace of the old woman in the girl—steps in, and between the three of them, they manage to get her to her feet. Until now, Alicia has seen a large number of younger girls, and some around her age, but the group she finds herself in the middle of is an exception: most of them must be fifty, sixty, older. The oldest—seventy-something, her hair dyed and cut short like a man's—asks if she's OK and holds out a bottle of water that's gone warm, and she also asks if she's planning to meet up with friends. Alicia looks at the teenager's T-shirt—WOMEN OF BLESSED BREAD... UNITE!—white Comic Sans on purple. She says no, she's going home, she just got off work and came out of curiosity.

"Less curiosity, more solidarity!" she hears someone behind her say. The old woman's expression is friendly, there's a little dark mole on her chin: in her speech, Alicia notices some of the echoes—vanishing consonants, open vowels—that she herself worked so hard to neutralize. "You can come along with us," she offers, while Alicia keeps looking at that chin; not at the mole, but the chin.

A woman falls to the ground. Several faltering steps, followed by her clutching at the arm of a woman with her back turned, the shoulder of a boy holding a poster, and when her legs fail her and she collapses, her body rebounds against several surrounding bodies on the way down. The other women react instinctively, moving apart, making space, stepping back when the woman hits the concrete; the body, the fall, the weakness, have generated a shockwave. Before anyone else reacts, María goes to help her up; she can't do it on her own, the woman weighs too much, so she and one of the younger girls try. They manage all together, with the woman shaking off the dizziness and making an effort herself. Are you OK, have some water, are you meeting friends: María strings together questions. Maybe she walked from another neighbourhood, like them, several hours together coming up from the south of the city, joining other women from other districts, and fell behind, her mobile phone dead, and lost the rest of her group.

Back at the association, it had seemed like a beautiful idea: not going straight to the station to meet, but walking en masse from the neighbourhood where they live, the neighbour-hood they've been working for, joining women they may not know, but who spend hours at their own associations, filling out forms, looking for solutions to other women's problems. That's how Laura described it when she told the others: we'll leave from here, from the square, where we'll also hand out flyers starting in the morning, and we'll tell every woman who stops about our demands, and the ones who don't stop, too, and any men who will listen.

We can give empowerment workshops, the ones in the younger group suggested, and María thought the word might put women off if they weren't used to that kind of language; María generally got the feeling that her messages weren't reaching those women, older women who no longer needed to care but to be cared for, immigrant women, Romani women, the women whose bodies didn't show up in the photos they shared on social media. But in the end, she thought, in the end, that had to do with power, too, and it had to do with money. Someone had to be earning it, someone had to look out for themselves first, in order to then share the proceeds with everyone else.

The woman says no, that to get home, she needs to go back to the metro; when she speaks, she makes an effort to enunciate every sound, not cut off a single plural, not miss a participle, ashamed of her accent. Several women from the group lay into her after that, but by then, María has stopped listening and has fixed her gaze on her: the very pale face, which could be the result of light-headedness; the small, dark eyes; the physique of someone who's stopped taking care of herself, flesh pudgy and soft; the chin riddled with spots, and a hair or two. For a moment, María thinks: the chin. Are those the eyes that contain my memory, first his, then hers: how different my life would have been if I'd never seen them. She's not a girl: the woman who hands back the water bottle must already be thirty-something. And she is trying to leave, thanking them, moving off; in her voice, there's a certain urgency, a nervousness. María makes a final attempt, not so she'll continue on with them, but so she'll offer some piece of information: her exact age, her name, the background she's trying to hide. My name's María, what's yours? And then she might at least find out that much. Maybe her name is Alicia or Eva. Judging by the age, she'd be Alicia, the one who Chico says is so smart and so standoffish, the one who took the father's death the hardest. But María notices the ring on her right hand; Chico would have told her, he would have at least told her that, she thinks, as much as she has said for so long that she doesn't want to hear anything. As far as she knows, neither of Carmen's daughters is married. The woman stops, she turns towards María, she doesn't answer. María smiles, says goodbye, wishes the woman luck—and, in some way, the woman is thereby vouchsafed good luck. María breathes a sigh of relief: no, that's not Alicia, it's not Eva. She got carried away, that's all.

Seriously? In the old woman's chin, she thought she recognized her own, which has always bothered her so much: Alicia, she warns herself, don't overthink. How many poorly sculpted chins have you come across in all these years? Alicia has seen lots of uneven chins like that, and it never occurred to her that she was connected to them by anything more than the joke their bodies had played. While she walks aimlessly on, down to Santa María de la Cabeza—she'll end up coming out near the river, on the other side of the city—Alicia tries hard to imagine the scene in which her father, barely more than a teenager, convinced her teenage mother—yes, she was still in her teens—that maybe it wasn't such a good idea to name their daughter after the woman she hated: Alicia would have been called María, if her mother had her way. In which case, the baby Alicia sometimes imagines would be Carmencita, after the woman who ruined her own life: greedy monster, the clothing she wore and the food she ate paid for with the sweat of Alicia's father, and the blood that stains his suit in her dreams every night. Life could have treated Alicia well: private school in a good neighbourhood, a prestigious university, a guaranteed job in the family business. What has it given her instead, she wonders as she approaches a guy on a bench, consulting his phone; if he's not interested, she'll have no choice but to go down to Marqués de Vadillo and see what she can find. That's what she needs right now: another name, another job, a good time, for a few hours at least. She'll come up with some excuse for Nando. Alicia tells herself again and again and again: whoever you are, old lady, I'm no one to you. Cross me out like something you jotted down on a supermarket coupon: one line, and I don't exist any more. Old lady, your accent, your chin: I don't exist.

By the time Alicia opens the door to her apartment, Nando is already sprawled in the middle of the bed, snoring, arms and legs outstretched, as if pointing the way: as if saying, get out. Alicia had first made use of her co-worker's delay, and lied to Nando, sending him a WhatsApp saying that her co-worker had failed to find childcare after all and had asked Alicia to fill in for her. Don't be too nice, Nando reminded her; give them an inch, people take a mile. I scratch my back, you scratch mine, Alicia replied, with an exceptional emoji that allows you to send a kiss and a heart at the same time. By 10 p.m. she should have sent some sort of reply to all his messages, are you getting off on time, when are you getting off, how are you, is everything OK, I'll meet you at the metro. At midnight she turned off her phone so the screen wouldn't even light up every time Nando called her.

Alicia didn't know how to lie: she smelt of alcohol and not, she hoped, vomit; she'd only dry-vomited into the toilet twice. She took off her clothes and tried to fit into a small gap next to him on the bed. He sensed her, moved away, yielded half the mattress. Alicia, the second time you came over. Do you remember? Yes, she said. I asked you to be gentle with me. That was your end of the deal. You aren't sticking to it.

That girl who fell down at Atocha next to our group, María thinks. It was strange: at first, I noticed her way of speaking, hiding the accent; how she forced the "s", the "d", and it pained me that she would feel so much shame about wherever it was she came from. But then I saw her chin, shapeless like mine. I worked out her age, and I thought she could be my eldest granddaughter. I know nothing about her—I asked my brother not to tell me anything, not to show me pictures. I've never tried looking for her, but suddenly: maybe just today, suddenly, we were meant to find each other. María listened to her friends talking, she tried to distract herself. There were still hours before they got to the end of the protest, and by the time the women from the neighbourhoods furthest away from the centre funnelled into Plaza de España, the lights and the music had already been turned off. Many complained of exhaustion, pain; others insisted they weren't even supposed to go on public transport. María told them, I worked just around the corner from here for years, in an apartment that belonged to a mother and her daughter. The mother died on me, I was alone with her, it was the day they buried

Franco, the daughter out attending the funeral in Valle de los Caídos. Then what happened, María? Nothing. I stayed on a few weeks more, and she stopped needing me. The youngest girls walked home, a journey of several hours. María, Laura, and some of the others went up to Argüelles to catch the metro; sure, they grumbled, it's a consumer strike, but that doesn't mean it's supposed to consume us. If that was her, María thought, would I be willing to turn my life upside down for a stranger? María thinks about today and today alone: I have to take one day at a time. And she counts the stops left before she gets home, convinced that, no—she's sure of it—no.

María closes the door to her apartment. She turns on the light and takes her time moving through it, room to room. When she last renewed the lease, she joked with her landlord, the grandson of the woman she had first rented it from: when you show it to the next tenant, you can tell them the last one took such good care of the place that you let her die here. He took it in his stride, said: come on, that'll be years from now. Her dog is asleep in the living room, old and tired as she is; she decided to call her Lady. The couch has been reupholstered several times, and she swapped the old TV for a new one last Christmas, on a whim; the bedroom has been the same for years, decades; not a single ornament on the bedside table. In the living room, she put up shelves for her library: she feels proud paying for her own books, putting them out so anyone who comes into her home can see. Her sight is getting worse all the time, and she struggles with the small type. Everything that's happened, was it worth it? Everything, from the start: leaving nothing out. Today, for example: all the way up to arriving home, closing the door, turning on the living-room lamp. The rent for her tiny apartment. Her sofa. Her shelves. Her TV. María decides to sit down, to rest a while.